THE STAR TREK®
SKETCHBOOK
THE ORIGINAL SERIES

BY HERBERT F. SOLOW
& YVONNE FERN SOLOW

POCKET BOOKS
New York   London   Toronto   Sydney   Tokyo   Singapore

An *Original* Publication of POCKET BOOKS

POCKET BOOKS, a division of Simon & Schuster Inc.
1230 Avenue of the Americas, New York, NY 10020

Copyright © 1997 by Paramount Pictures. All Rights Reserved.

STAR TREK is a Registered Trademark of Paramount Pictures.

This book is published by Pocket Books,
a division of Simon & Schuster Inc.,
under exclusive license from Paramount Pictures.

ISBN: 0-671-00219-8

First Pocket Books trade paperback printing May 1997

10 9 8 7 6 5 4 3 2 1

POCKET and colophon are registered trademarks of
Simon & Schuster Inc.

Graphic Design: Laurie Goldman, Red Herring Design

Printed in the U.S.A.

For orders other than by individual consumers, Pocket Books grants a discount on the pur-
chase of **10 or more** copies of single titles for special markets or premium use. For further
details, please write to the Vice-President of Special Markets, Pocket Books, 1633
Broadway, New York, NY 10019-6785, 8th Floor.

For information on how individual consumers can place orders, please write to Mail Order
Department, Simon & Schuster Inc., 200 Old Tappan Road, Old Tappan, NJ 07675.

This book deals with four visionary artists; four men who had to create things that had never been created before; four men who took the written word and made it live. And over thirty years later, it is living still.

Every motion-picture film and every television show ends with what is known in the entertainment industry as "the credit roll" or "the end credits." This is an expanded list of all those individuals or companies who contributed to the making of that particular production. Most people who are not involved with the entertainment business rarely read these end credits. Consequently the tens upon tens, sometimes even hundreds upon hundreds, of people without whom the production simply could not be made are left unnoticed, unheralded, and unappreciated.

Even fewer people read the somewhat strange captions that describe what roles those individuals and those companies performed or supplied. And understandably, it is almost impossible for the average viewer to fathom what every contributor does, just from reading a title—like, for example, craft service man/woman, gaffer, standby painter, wrangler, grip, best boy, foley artist—et cetera.

Even without reading them, you know the credit roll/end credits tell you one thing: they tell you that an awful lot of people make contributions to and are responsible for everything that is in the motion picture or television episode that you've just seen. That's even more evident if the show you saw was a pilot episode, which is a research and development tool—the very beginning of a television series. In a pilot episode, every *thing* that you saw—every *thing* that you heard—will have an impact on the creative and visual fate of every future episode of that television series. If a particular television series has entertained and engaged its audience to such a high degree that a studio's good business judgment dictates a move from the small screen to the large screen, that motion picture is irrevocably tied to those fundamental sights and sounds that were created, developed, and constructed in the original television pilot film.

This is particularly true with noncontemporary series, especially true with futuristic series. And it was definitely true with *Star Trek*.

IN THE FOLLOWING PAGES, FOR THE FIRST TIME YOU WILL MEET THE VISUAL MINDS OF FOUR ARTISTS.

Walter "Matt" Jefferies, Jr., production designer/art director—Matt gave us the physical look of the *Enterprise* and the *Star Trek* universe. **William Ware Theiss**, costume designer—Bill designed and created the clothes of the *Star Trek* universe. **Frederick Beauregard Phillips**, makeup artist—Fred's makeup artistry made the *Star Trek* universe more human—and less human. **Wah Min Chang**, artist and model maker—Wah created and built many of the aliens and much of the gadgetry of *Star Trek*'s universe. You have never seen a screen credit on *Star Trek* for Wah Chang. But among the credit roll/end credits can be found the name of a company—Projects Unlimited. Projects Unlimited was owned by Wah Chang and Gene Warren, Sr. Both men had distinguished careers in the Hollywood special and optical effects world: Warren organizing and running the business, Wah imagining and building his creations. But Hollywood was always a strong labor town, and union disputes, union jurisdictions, and union competitiveness prevented Wah from receiving the public credit he deserved.

Of course, before these four men were hired and asked to expand their minds "galactically," there had to be a first step — a beginning. There was. It was an idea. An idea which led to the visual contributions of Matt, Bill, Freddy, and Wah

It started in April of 1964, when I hired Gene Roddenberry. When Gene arrived, I worked hand in hand with him, developing his *Star Trek* idea. There were but two of us—and there remained but two of us until I convinced Grant Tinker and Jerry Stanley at NBC that investing money in a *Star Trek* pilot script was a good move. Our ranks grew to four people, as Grant and Jerry contributed thoughts and ideas about Captain Pike's first adventure in the galaxy aboard the *U.S.S. Yorktown*, later the *U.S.S. Enterprise*.

The writing of the first pilot script brought in an "unofficial contributor" in Sam Peeples. Sam, well-versed in science fiction, space travel, and television pilot scripts, looked over Gene's shoulder with both a keen and a creative eye and joined the guiding fathers of *Star Trek*.

When the pilot script and my persistence at NBC brought us an order for the production of the pilot film, our ranks swelled many fold—well before we shot a foot of film. The "below-the-line" or nuts and bolts depart-

represented by a clock, the actors come on board in the last three minutes. Ninety-five percent of every production is accomplished before the actors even know it exists. In the case of the *Star Trek* pilot, they were the secondary crew, the one that propelled the *Enterprise* in and out of warp drive. But first came the primary crew, the one that made *Star Trek* look like *Star Trek*—they were next up.

The primary *Star Trek* crew were the designers. These were film-experienced, highly qualified visual architects charged with designing a very complicated living structure—a structure truly as complicated as the tallest skyscraper.

Without this primary crew, the *Enterprise* and everything else associated with *Star Trek* would never fly. Without them there would be no ship

ments at the studio, production and budget, took our script, "broke it down" into areas, and projected what each and every area would cost: camera, lighting, set construction, props, wardrobe, makeup, special effects, and more. Then each area had its own breakdown and rebreakdown of necessary people and projected costs. Set construction became labor and materials, and further became costs of specific manpower and wood and nails and canvas and paint. The preparation of the pilot was under way. We were then about twenty people.

What about the actors? Those most prominent names on the credit roll? Well, if a one-hour television episode is

The primary *Star Trek* crew were the designers.

to propel. There would actually be nothing to wear, nothing to use, nothing to see. So only after the designers turned our ideas into objects did we supply the actors. Then, and only then, did their time come—just before we were ready to shoot that first foot of film.

The time of the birth of *Star Trek*, in 1964, was also the time of the massive growth of color television—a factor which had a very strong impact both on *Star Trek* getting on the air and on its "color look."

RCA, the parent company of NBC, had won the "battle of the color systems." Their black and white compatible color transmission system bested the CBS Laboratories' incompatible black and white color system and was approved by a committee of the Federal Communications Commission. NBC, then owned by RCA, was similarly charged with becoming the first full-color network, because without television color programming, consumers weren't about to pay the high cost of an RCA color television set.

NBC set a threefold approach to acquiring color television series. One was to produce their own series in color, like *Bonanza*. However, according to David Dortort, the producer-writer of *Bonanza*, it was also his financial contribution that initially put *Bonanza* into color.

NBC's second approach was to convert all their current black and white programming into color. The approach was quite simple. All suppliers of programs to NBC were offered—an offer you did not want to refuse lest an early cancellation await your show—an additional $7500 per hour over and above your black and white program price. Based on what NBC was paying for black and white programming those days, the $7500 per hour amounted to an increase of anywhere from 5 percent to 10 percent of the program price.

NBC's third approach, the approach that clearly helped boost *Star Trek* onto the NBC schedule, was to initiate original color television series. *Star Trek*, a series that invited NBC viewers to journey, through the literary brilliance of America's best science-fiction writers, into the color brilliance of the galaxy, was at the right place at the right time.

4

Motion-picture companies had been making color films for well over thirty years and had been doing so extremely well. They knew that what you saw in the projection room, you saw on the motion-picture screen. Colors were true from the filmmaking process to exhibition. But that wasn't so for this new medium. Some colors changed when transmitted—Mr. Spock's yellow skin became green. Some colors were unreadable—actually gold lettering was the most readable. Some colors were too harsh; some colors "bled" into other colors; some colors were too "hot"—others were too "cold."

Enter *Star Trek*'s film-experienced, highly qualified visual architects — Matt, Bill, Freddie, and Wah. We hired them not only to create the visuals of *Star Trek* but to do so under the guidelines of this new medium—the electrical transmission of color images.

What they did and how they did it is the central theme of this book. They did not deal in words, but rather in a visual cornucopia of textures, materials, light refraction, hues, shapes, movement, form, and so on. Their story is best told, not in words, but rather in the way they told it. Here, for the first time, we'll tell their story their way: with images.

HERE, FOR THE FIRST TIME, WE'LL TELL THEIR STORY THEIR WAY: WITH IMAGES.

So when you have seen this book, other words will have more meaning for you: those end credits on the first *Star Trek* pilot, the second pilot, and the original series—and every other program or movie you see. The next time you see the names Walter "Matt" Jefferies, William Ware Theiss, Fred Phillips, and Wah Chang (Projects Unlimited), you will think of four of the real creators of *Star Trek*.

Herbert F. Solow
Malibu, California
November 1996

Science-fiction set and prop designers, costumers, and makeup artists have a unique task: to portray that which we have never seen. The creative teams of *Star Trek* and its subsequent incarnations are extraordinary. From sets to make-up, from costumes to props, the visual *Star Trek* universe is regenerated daily. As a result, we speak of a *Star Trek* event as having happened, rather than merely having been seen. "Remember when Edith Keeler died?" we are likely to say, as though it were part of a shared past experience—which, in a sense, it is. The *Star Trek* experience continues to thrive, not only because of its inherent philosophy, but because of the imagination, dedication, and sheer excellence of its creative team.

Depicted below are the signature works of our four artists—those creations which both represent the physical appearance, and manifest the spirit of all of Star Trek.

Yvonne Fern Solow
Malibu, California
November 1996

THE ENTERPRISE
designed by Walter M. Jefferies, 1965

U.S.S. Enterprise, NCC 1701, was launched in 2245, and made its television debut 279 years earlier, on September 8, 1966. But the name *Enterprise* dates back even further—to the times of wooden sailing ships. Since then, there have been an aircraft carrier, a space shuttle, and finally Captain Kirk's *Constitution*-class vessel.

More than any other artifact created for the series, the *Enterprise* represents *Star Trek*. It is truly as much a character as Mr. Spock. And like its human (or organic) counterparts, it has changed its shape, but never its name; changed its capabilities, but never its mission; changed its crew, but never its character.

The *Enterprise* theoretically travels through space at many times the speed of light. At such high velocities, the ship would be literally torn apart by even the smallest piece of debris. It became clear to spacefaring cultures at a very early stage that some system for eliminating such debris must be devised. From this need came focused energy emitters. These devices vaporize or ionize tiny particles in the ship's path, leaving a clear trajectory along which it can safely travel. Naturally it wasn't long before someone made the leap of logic to conclude that such focused-energy devices, if several times more powerful, could be used as weapons. From this the Phaser was born. The name derives from the acronym for PHASed Energy Rectification, the process through which energy is transformed and focused on a target. (This, of course, takes place in the fictional world. In reality, Matt Jefferies designed the ship's phasers—and the hand phaser, which is his favorite prop.)

From its inception to its demise, Matt Jefferies's *Enterprise* has been beloved by millions of people. This mythical ship has inspired passionate devotion for over thirty years.

6

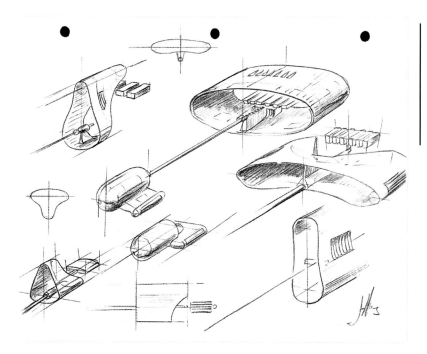

Here is the first moment of the *U.S.S. Enterprise*: the embryonic ship—the first sketch made to depict what the Wagon Train to the stars would look like. Hundreds of sketches followed, many of which are reproduced in this book. However, this is the very first to be labeled *U.S.S. Enterprise*.

(Opposite page)
The final sketch, from which the model for the show was made, can be called the "birth" of the *Enterprise*. It was this drawing that Desilu Studio Vice President and Executive in Charge of the entire production of *Star Trek*, Herb Solow, approved for production, giving the final go-ahead to the producer and the creative team.

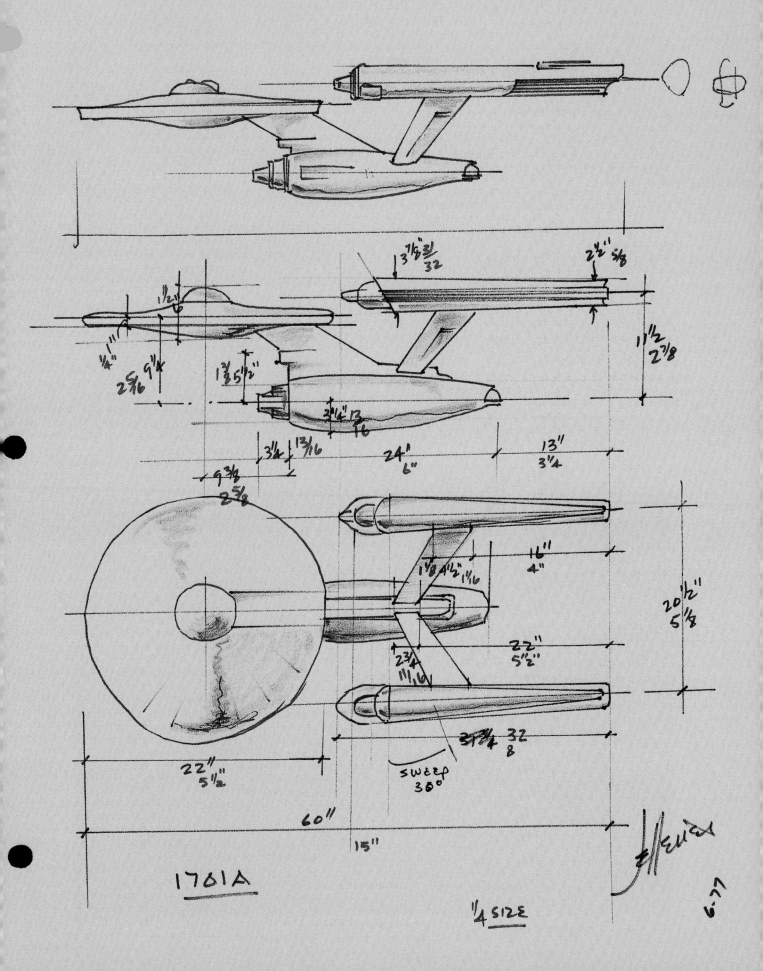

1701A   ¼ SIZE

THE SALT VAMPIRE
constructed by Wah Chang, 1965

A familiar face, captured in its final days both as a species and as an individual, the salt monster, also known as the salt vampire, is the last of its kind. Haunting, lonely, and fatal, the doomed shapeshifter meets its end at the hand of the one who most wants to save it, the gentle Leonard McCoy. "The Man Trap" is a tragic tale, in which beauty and the beast are one and the same. The salt monster is no mugato. As its only friend, Dr. Robert Crater heatedly defends it to Kirk: "It's not just a beast! It is intelligent." The

salt creature's intelligence, however, neither prevents nor compensates for its addiction, and like the beast Captain Kirk claims it to be, it kills—for a few grams of sodium chloride.

"The Man Trap," written by George Clayton Johnson, was the first *Star Trek* episode aired, though the sixth produced, and the characters were still in a shakedown period. In later episodes, Kirk was to show much more compassion for other life-forms.

The intention here no doubt was to show him as a fearless, dedicated leader, who would go to any lengths to protect his crew. However, being *Star Trek*, "The Man Trap" gives us a glimpse of the other side—of pitiable alienness and silent fear.

Wah Chang's subtle and delicate molding of emotional texture into what could have been merely a crude monster-figure draws us into tender alliance with "strange new worlds."

8

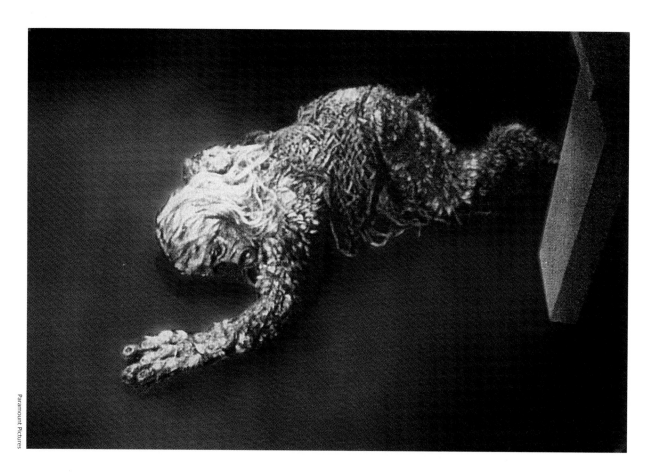

SPOCK'S EARS

created by Fred Phillips, 1965

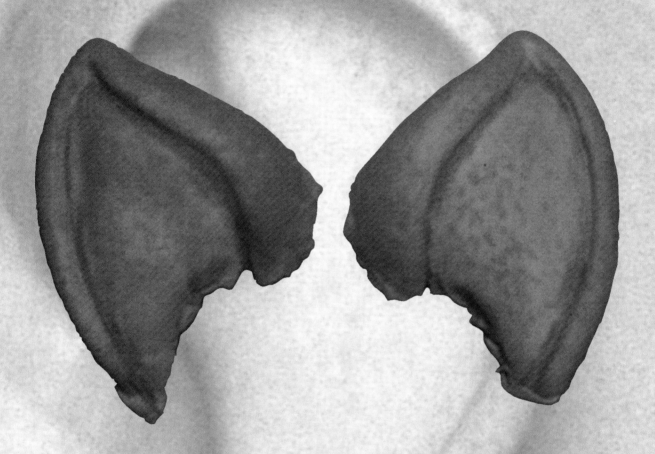

Who does not see him- or herself reflected in the many-faceted alien, Mr. Spock? More than any other character in *Star Trek*, Spock has been examined, analyzed, and discussed—and found to be, in his own word, "fascinating." Now almost a cult figure, Spock is a brilliant portrait of the entire spectrum of human/alien existence.

At a time and in a place where pointed ears could easily represent evil, Spock emerged—ethical, honest, compassionate, intelligent—and with auditory apparatus that was definitely diabolic.

Enough has been written about Spock's ears in various publications to fill a book. However, as symbols, these infamous extensions represent one of *Star Trek's* most significant messages: "To be different is not necessarily to be ugly—to have a different idea is not necessarily to be wrong."

Fred Phillips, veteran makeup artist, with a dedication born of long experience in the family business, worked tirelessly around the clock to shape, mold, refine, and invent comfortable, reusable ears for Leonard Nimoy. The monumental obstacles to that end, given the materials of the day, made him realize that coming up with any ears that would not fall off during shooting was all that he could hope for. Nevertheless, Mr. Spock owes his first television appearance as a Vulcan to Fred Phillips.

The single most important reason that *Star Trek* became a television show was the idea that Starfleet was parallel to the U.S. Navy. What Herb Solow, Vice President of Desilu, liked about *Star Trek*, from the first, single piece of paper he was given by Roddenberry, was that the roles of the characters and structure of shipboard

STARFLEET UNIFORMS
designed by William Ware Theiss, 1965

life were recognizable, organized, and clear. This made it salable to the people at NBC who would have to put up the money to make the pilot. Plus it would be readily identifiable to the general audience.

Gene Roddenberry many years later acknowledged that the idea for Starfleet came from Robert Heinlein's *Space Cadet*. It was that idea of a uniformed service that was given to William Ware (Bill) Theiss. The uniforms therefore not only became a visual signature for *Star Trek* to the viewing public, but also were a representation of a standard of ethics embodied by Starfleet and the people who wore the uniform.

"Narrow focus" is how Bill Theiss described his work. "I went to work in the morning and spent every moment trying to come up with ideas that would look futuristic and otherworldly. I wasn't a big science-fiction fan—and I didn't know anything about the meaning of anything. I just wanted it all to work, visually and artistically."

11

In an age when normal business attire—even military attire—included starched materials, drab colors, and neckties, this glimpse into the garments of the 23rd century was dramatic and futuristic.

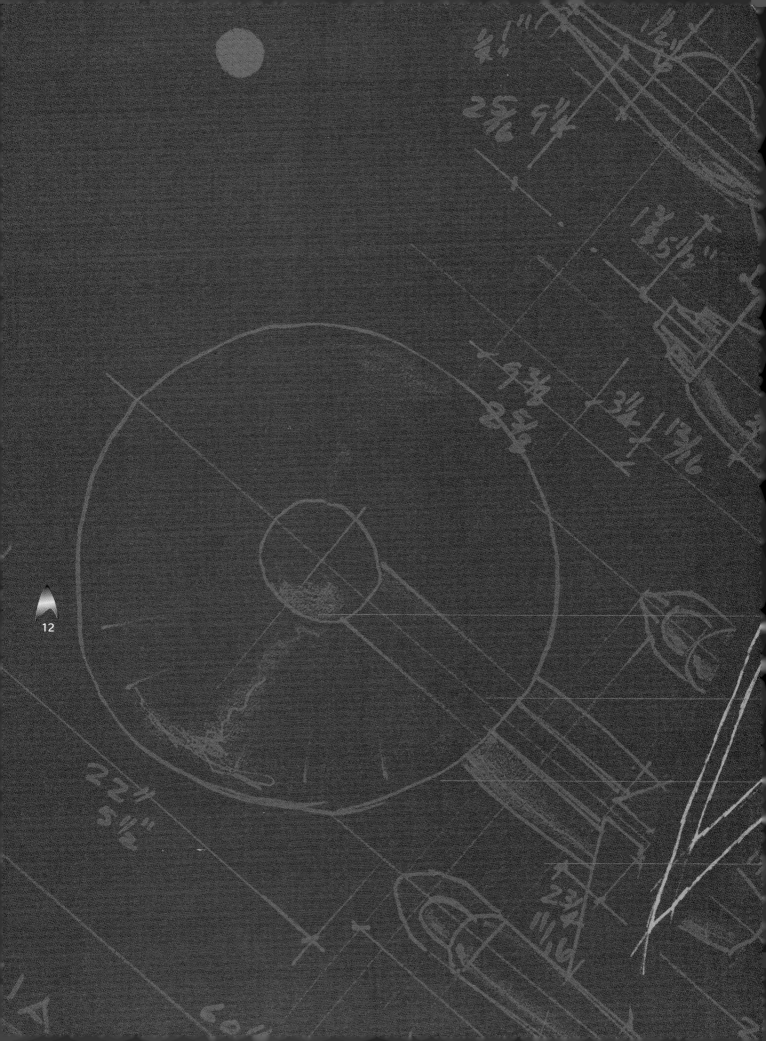

12

CONTENTS

WALTER MATTHEW JEFFERIES

Matt Jefferies's 1935 Waco airplane

The biplane flew overhead in the shimmering heat, its trailing banner snapping sharply. The familiar drone of the engine brought the party outside —all of the party-goers crowding onto the patio of the Santa Paula Airport restaurant, straining to catch the first glimpse of the 1935 Waco airplane, wing identification number NC17740, and its streamer message. A murmur rippled through the group—assembled from across the country for this special event—as the little plane came into view. Many took out their cameras. Others read the message aloud: "Happy 75th Birthday, Matt/Walt/Jeff."

Walter Matthew Jefferies, known to family, friends, and colleagues by all three names, celebrated the weekend of his birthday in his second home— the hangar at the Santa Paula Airport—with his wife, MaryAnn, and dozens of family members and friends.

"I got into the business by being a specialist," Matt says. "I was a mechanical artist and there happened to be a need for one at Warner Bros. on *Bombers B52*, where my brother was working. Then they needed a mechanical shark for *The Old Man and the Sea*, so I laid out a twenty-eight-

14

foot shark. Then I laid out some ship interiors for them—I forget what for—and later I did some at MGM for *Wreck of the Mary Deare*. I also did some aircraft interiors for Sinatra's *Never So Few*. Then it was on to Desilu for some work on *The Untouchables*. From there, one thing led to another, and I was hired by Herb for *Star Trek*.

"*Star Trek* was nothing like anything before. Coming up with ideas was the biggest problem. I liked Gene [Roddenberry], but he was really a dreamer. I was a nuts and bolts man. I guess we were a good balance! 'Sure,' I'd tell Gene, 'we'll have doors and glasses and forks in a few hundred years, but what will they look like? What will they be made of? And what about things we don't have now—phasers and so on? What do they look like?' There just weren't enough hours in a day or a week for me. On the pilot, they were filming on one part of the set and I was chalking in another part at the same time."

Designing for a show, Matt says, "Basically, you've got to satisfy the producers—for *Star Trek*, it was Gene and Herb; you've got to satisfy the studio; you've got to satisfy the network that's putting up the money; and you've got to keep the director happy. If he doesn't like what you've created, you stand a good chance of not getting the show finished on

Courtesy Herbert F. Solow

time. It's also got to work for the cameraman and the soundman, too. On top of all that, you've got to deliver it on time and for the money. If it looks good, that's a plus. But those other requirements have to be met first. You can come up with the most beautiful design in the world, but if you can't deliver it on time and within budget, you've blown it. As far as I'm concerned, if something looked good on that show, it was an accident, because the other concerns were more important."

Matt's contribution obviously was no accident—it was the result of meticulously applied talent and industry over more hours per day than now seems humanly possible. Although he went on to design such visible and successful series as *Love, American Style*, *The Little House on the Prairie*, and *Dallas*,

he will always be remembered as the designer of the most phenomenal science-fiction series of all time.

Star Trek owes its visual identity and its profound gratitude to Walter M. Jefferies, who celebrated his 75th birthday in 1996, the year *Star Trek* turned 30.

The Episodes

Creating a new set every week was a daunting task, largely because of lead time.

Lead time, the time between the scheduling of the production of an episode and the actual commencement of filming on that episode, varied on *Star Trek* between two and, in very rare cases, five weeks. But whatever it was, it was never enough time for the design process. Because Matt carried the overall responsibility for the look of the series, it was imperative that he be given as much lead time as possible.

The issuing of scripts, first drafts, changes, and final drafts was based on need. Actors usually got their scripts last. For one thing, they were busy working on the currently shooting episode. But more importantly, the less lead time the actors had, the less time they had to lobby and complain about the size, scope, or extent of their roles.

However, not only did Matt get his scripts with the first issuance—called the "yellow-cover white copy," which was given to key production and budget personnel, casting, wardrobe, NBC, and Solow—but Matt was given the writer's first-draft story, a practice rarely done on television series. Oddly, it was almost always done on *Star Trek*. It was the old adage at work: forewarned is forearmed.

It was a huge team effort, as Matt is quick to point out, yet the set design always began with the writers' ideas: transmitted, usually hastily, to Matt, who would begin another series of feverish hours sketching, thinking, measuring, resketching, consulting with the producers—and many times, the alternating directors Marc Daniels and Joe Pevney—then finalizing the sketches.

"Some of the sets were literally outlined on the floor with the toe of my boot," he recalls.

As much as he wanted to create exciting, high-quality sets for every episode, the time and budget constraints simply would not allow anything beyond a creative minimum. This was actually an asset in such surrealistic episodes as "The Empath" and "Spectre of the Gun." More often, however, an entire planned idea had to be eliminated because of scene or script changes or omissions.

Much that Matt designed never made it into three dimensions, as can be seen on the following pages, where a small sample of the thousands of Jefferies's drawings, needed to create the settings for *Star Trek*'s legendary journeys, tell their eloquent story.

Sulu heats a rock,
demonstrating the varying
power of the phasers, in
"The Enemy Within."

The engineering
power shaft first seen in
"The Enemy Within."

17

"What Are Little Girls Made Of?"
called for underground caverns, designed
to be foreboding and confining.

ANDROID LABORATORY
"WHAT LITTLE GIRLS ARE MADE OF"
#10

The android lab of the Old Ones, discovered by Roger Korby, also from "What Are Little Girls Made Of?"

An alien's idea of a typical Earth home: Trelane's manor from "The Squire of Gothos."

No detail was overlooked: one of the Air Force trophies seen for just a second in "Tomorrow Is Yesterday."

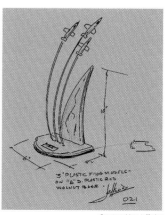

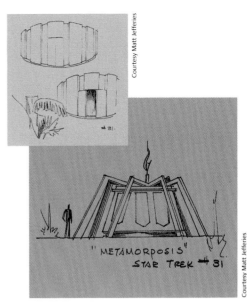

"Return of the Archons," where a culture was trying to survive the force of Landru in subterranean chambers.

Zefram Cochrane's survival housing created from the remains of his ship in "Metamorphosis."

A study for the matte painting done for "Errand of Mercy" noting where the sets would show, in the final version.

19

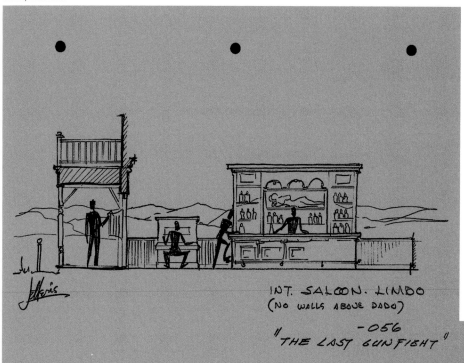

INT. SALOON. LIMBO
(NO WALLS ABOVE DADO)
-056
"THE LAST GUNFIGHT"

The interior of the half-formed saloon seen in "Spectre of the Gun."

Vaal, a computer disguised as a god, from "The Apple."

STAR TREK
"VAAL" FOR THE APPLE
SHOW 38

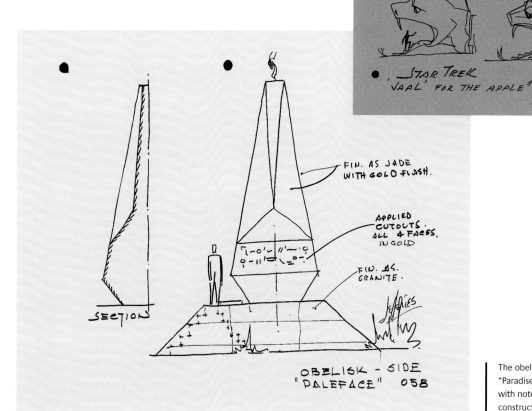

SECTION

FIN. AS JADE
WITH GOLD FLASH.

APPLIED
CUTOUTS.
ALL 4 FACES.
IN GOLD

FIN. AS.
GRANITE.

OBELISK - SIDE
"PALEFACE" 058

The obelisk created for "Paradise Syndrome," with notes to the construction department.

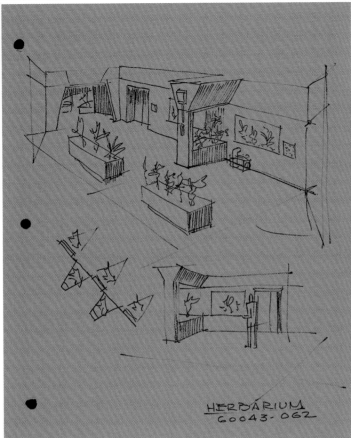

The stage plan for the herbarium.

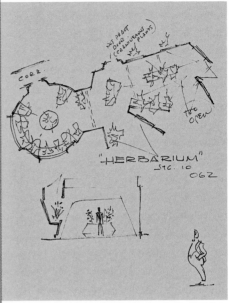

Doctor Miranda Jones's need to discover a rose called for the creation of a herbarium, in the episode "Is There in Truth No Beauty?"

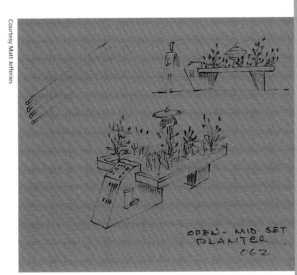

A close-up of a planter in the herbarium.

21

The habitat of Ambassador Kollos, an alien life-form so different that it needed its own environment, from "Is There in Truth No Beauty?"

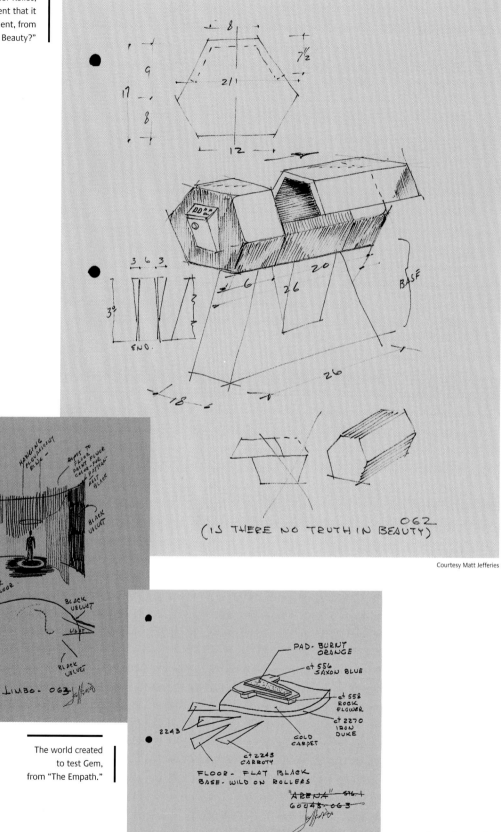

(IS THERE NO TRUTH IN BEAUTY)

The world created to test Gem, from "The Empath."

(opposite page)
The Oracle's room from "For the World is Hollow and I have Touched the Sky."

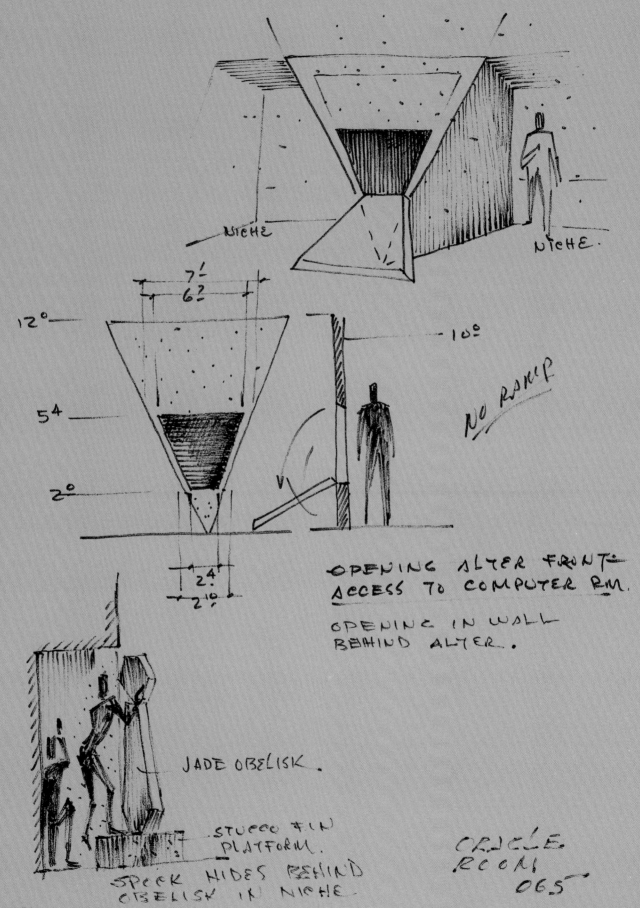

NICHE

NICHE.

7'
6'
12°
-10°
5⁴
NO RAMP
2°
2⁴
2¹⁰

OPENING ALTER FRONT.
ACCESS TO COMPUTER RM.

OPENING IN WALL
BEHIND ALTER.

JADE OBELISK.

STUCCO FIN
PLATFORM.

SPOCK HIDES BEHIND
OBELISK IN NICHE.

ORACLE
ROOM
065

SURFACE — INNER CORE
ASTEROID SPACE SHIP
OGS

Courtesy Matt Jefferies

To save a race, a spaceship was created to look like an asteroid. Upon discovering this, an old man spoke his last words, which served as the title.

The quarters of Natira, the priestess of the Oracle.

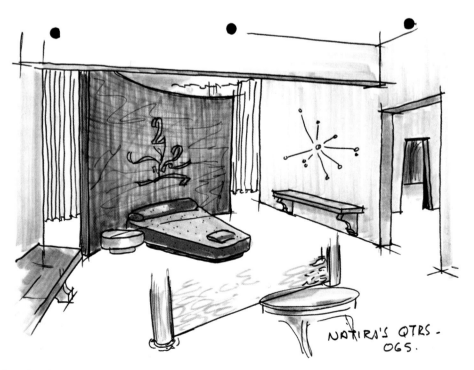

NATIRA'S QTRS.
OGS.

Courtesy Matt Jefferies

The altar of
the Oracle.

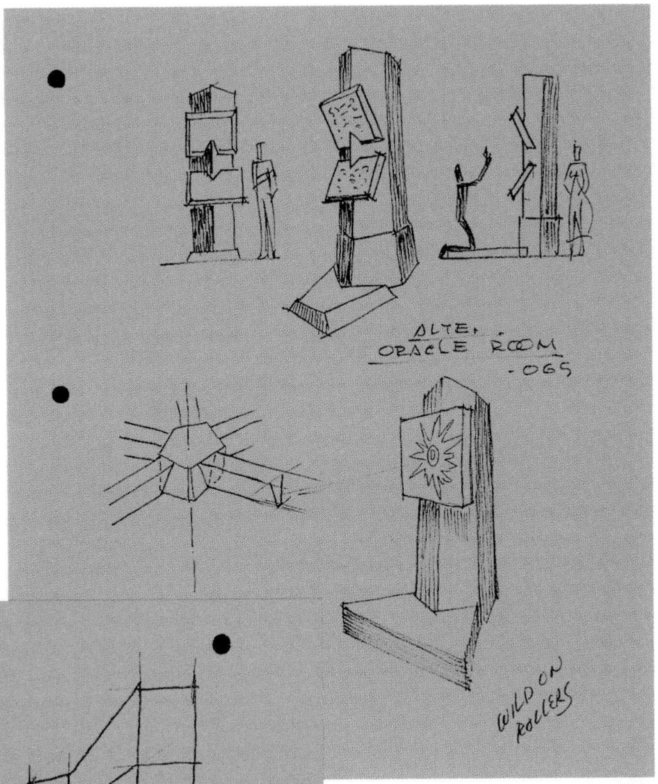

ALTE. ORACLE ROOM
·OGS

WILD ON ROLLERS

CONTROL ROOM
OGS

The control room that would
save the world Yonada.

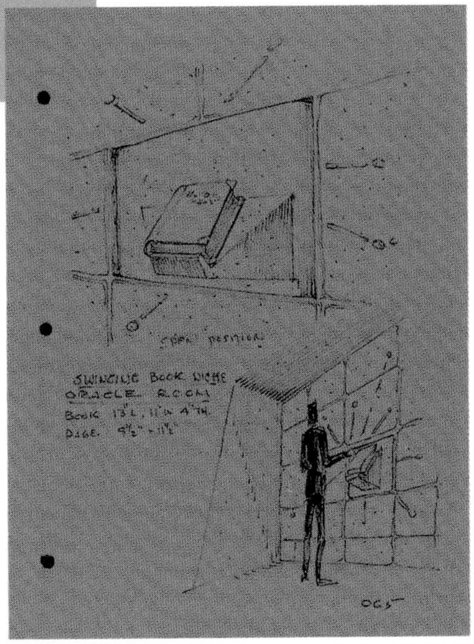

25

SWINGING BOOK NICHE
ORACLE ROOM

A close-up study of
the book niche.

The chamber of Parmen,
the self-styled leader of
"Plato's Stepchildren."

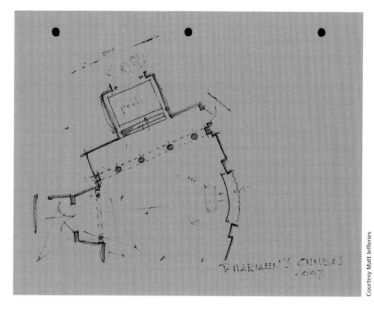

26

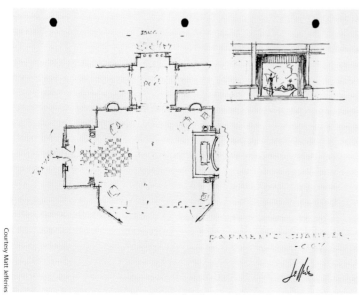

The stage plan of
Parmen's room.

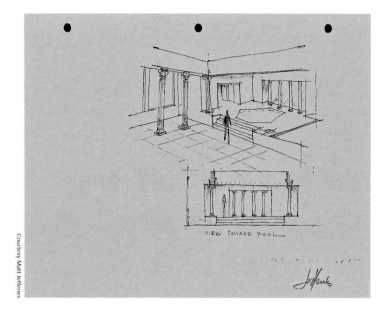

VIEW TOWARD POOL

The "court" of
the Platonians.

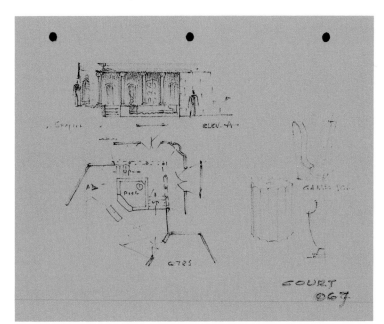

Stage plan of the court.

28

The audience box of
the colonnade.

"Wink of an Eye" was a "bottle" show with the need for only one set, a fountain.

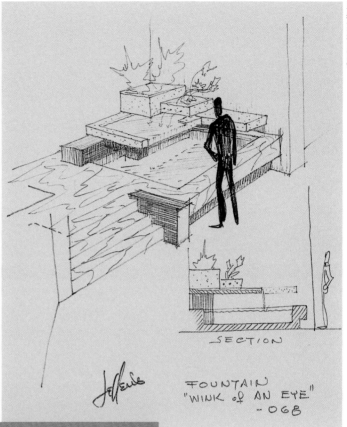

29

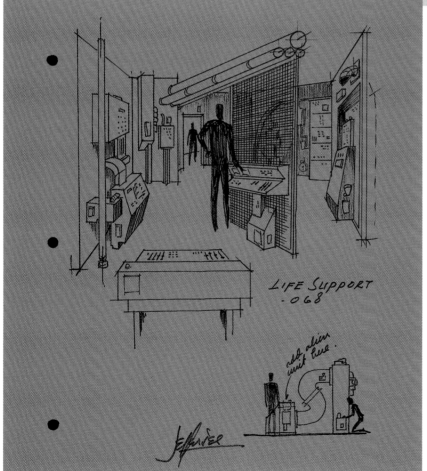

The Scalosians' life-support device, which was installed aboard the *Enterprise*.

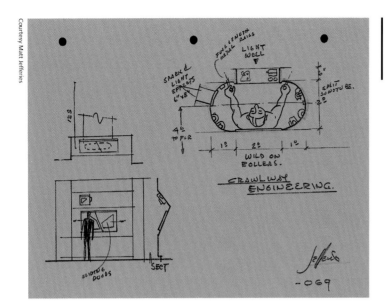

A new crawlway was created for "That Which Survives," to show where the matter and antimatter were mixed to power the ship's warp drive.

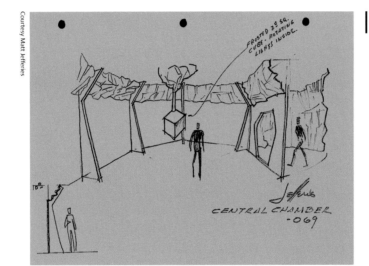

All that survived were a chamber and recording.

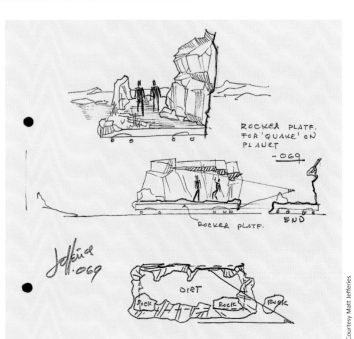

The exterior of the planet during a quake.

The dining room of the Federation rehab colony on Elba II, from "Whom Gods Destroy."

DINING ROOM -071

BACK WALL 489 FIELD STONE
HEADER 818 AQUA. MIST
SIDE WALLS 447 DESERT GRASS
REVEALS 418 JUNIPER
FLOORS 451 GORGE

LIGHT

SECTION THRU FORCE FIELD

CELL BLOCK -071
"WHO GODS DESTROY"

The cell block on the Elba colony.

The rehab colony's control room.

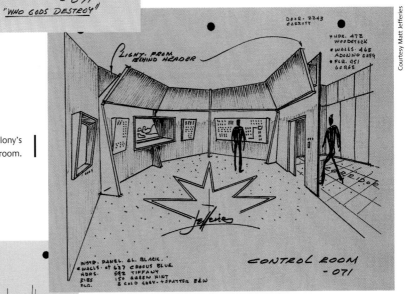

LIGHT FROM BEHIND HEADER

DOOR - 2243 GARROTY

HDR. 472 WOODSTOCK
WALLS 468 ADONNO GREY
FLR. 451 GORGE

INSTR. PANEL GL. BLACK.
WALLS 627 CROCUS BLUE
HDRG. 592 TIFFANY
RIBS 150 GREEN MINT
FLR. COLD GREY + SPATTER R&W

CONTROL ROOM -071

31

ELEV. B   OPEN   ELEV. A   OPEN

INT. DINING RM. 071

Construction and camera angles are laid out in the stage plan of the dining hall.

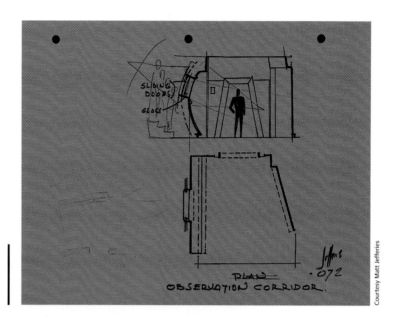

A re-dress of the observation corridor to show how the *Enterprise* was "re-created" on the surface of a planet, from "The Mark of Gideon."

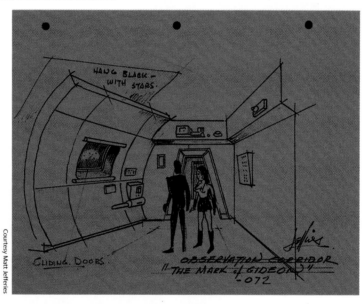

32

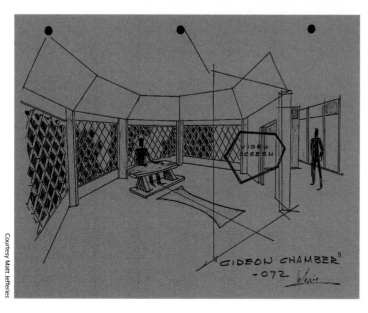

The council chamber on Gideon, showing the placement of the view screen.

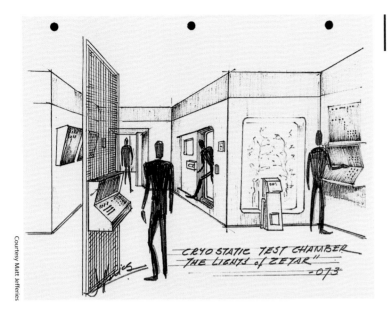

For "The Lights of Zetar": a proposed "cryo-static test chamber."

The pressure chamber in McCoy's lab used in "The Lights of Zetar."

Computer central.

33

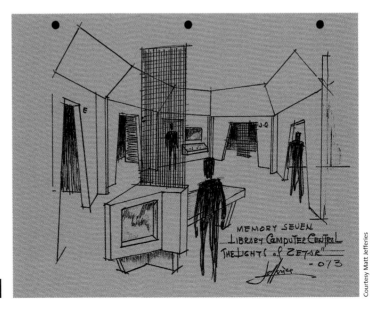

The library computer on Memory Alpha.

A gallery on the cloud city Stratos, from "The Cloud Minders."

The detention room.

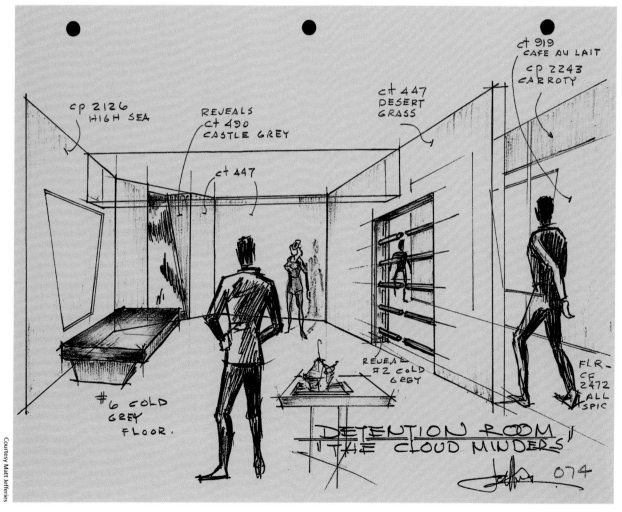

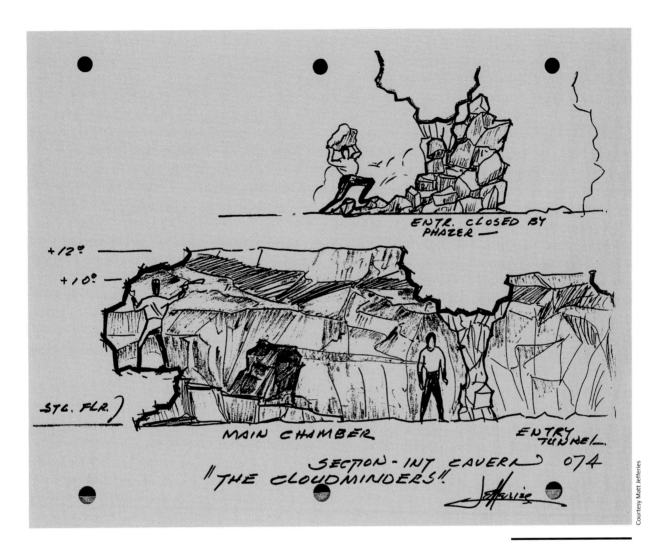

ENTR. CLOSED BY
PHAZER

+12°
+10°

STG. FLR.

MAIN CHAMBER

ENTRY
TUNNEL

SECTION - INT CAVERN 074
"THE CLOUDMINDERS"

On the planet below Stratos,
a cave where zenite was mined.

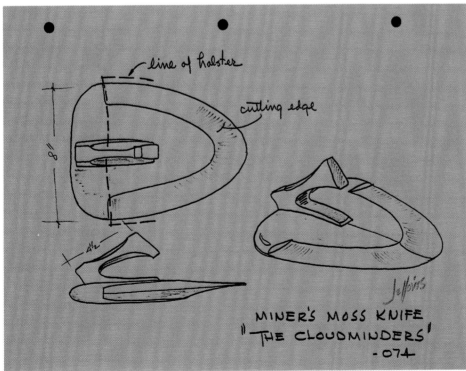

line of holster

cutting edge

8"

4½

MINER'S MOSS KNIFE
"THE CLOUDMINDERS"
-074

The knife used by the
Troglyte miners.

The proposed views
for the landing site
and the exterior of the
fabled planet Eden, from
"The Way to Eden."

The studio of a man who has lived many lives.

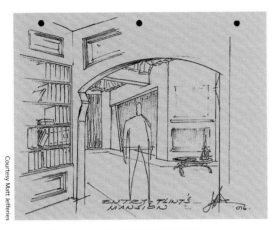

(Above, top)
Flint's mansion from "Requiem for Methuselah."

(Above, bottom)
A detail study of the entry to Flint's mansion.

Rayna's room.

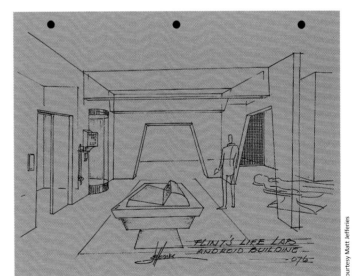

The lab where Flint created his android.

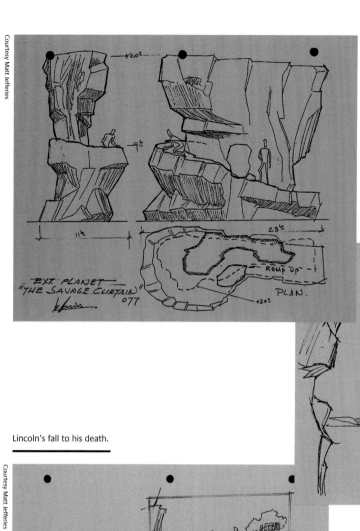

The hostile world of
the Excalbians, from
"The Savage Curtain."

Lincoln's fall to his death.

Kirk's base camp
on Excalbia.

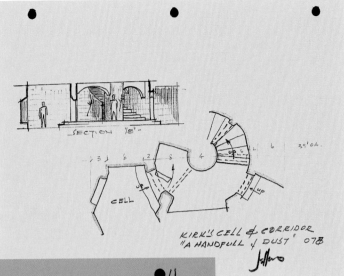

KIRK'S CELL & CORRIDOR
"A HANDFULL of DUST" 078

SECTION "1/8"-

CELL

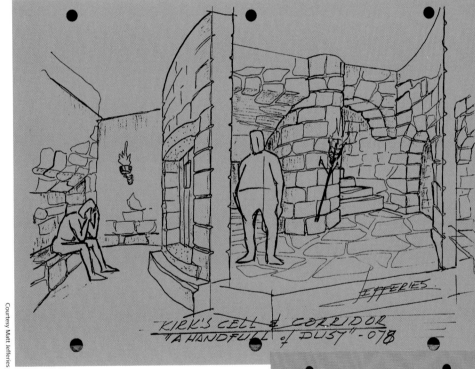

JEFFERIES

KIRK'S CELL & CORRIDOR
"A HANDFULL of DUST"-078

The views of Kirk's cell in the past of Sarpeidon, from "All Our Yesterdays."

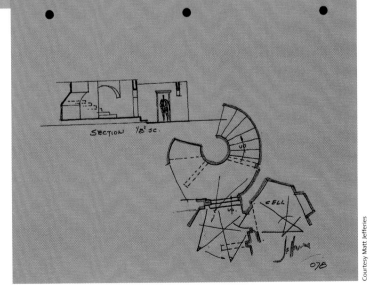

SECTION 1/8" SC.

CELL

078

DUNGEON CORRIDOR
"A HANDFUL of DUST" 078

A longer view of
Kirk's dungeon.

INT. LIBRARY
·078

The library of
Mr. Atoz.

40

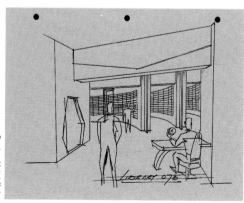

LIBRARY 078

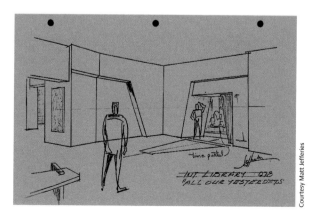

time portal

INT. LIBRARY 078
"ALL OUR YESTERDAYS"

Janice Lester "zaps" Kirk
to take his place, in
"Turnabout Intruder."

A detail of a chair at
the dig on Camus II.

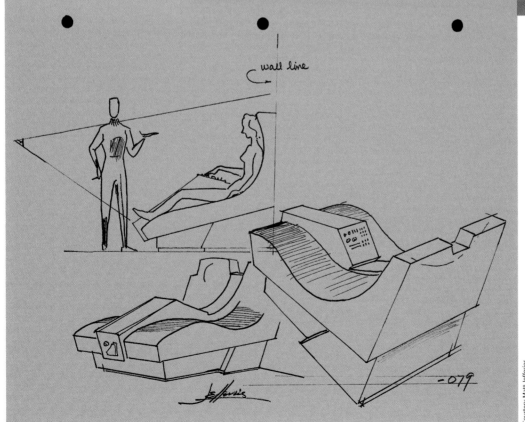

To move from a sketch to a three-dimensional set requires the talent and craftsmanship of carpenters, prop makers, painters, model makers, and a host of support staff. But it all has to begin with a few lines on a piece of paper before those efforts can result in a wall, a castle, a rock, an obelisk, a deity, a temple, or a city in the clouds.

Following are the scenes with which we are all familiar, and how they all began.

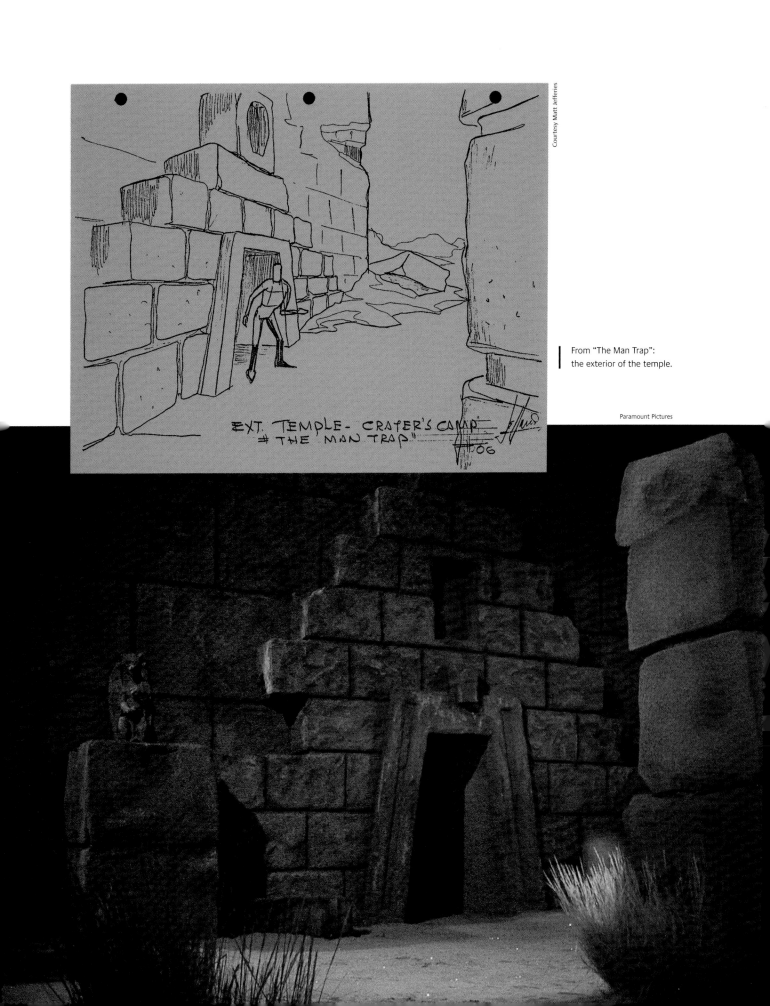

From "The Man Trap":
the exterior of the temple.

Professor Crater's camp,
also from "The Man Trap."

Scale: ¼" = 1'-0"

RUINS —
CRATERS CAMP
6149-6

HOR.

HOR.

STG.
FLR.

44

Trelane's manor, from "The Squire of Gothos."

45

CORRIDOR - TO HALL of AUDIENCES
"RETURN OF THE ARCHONS"
#22

The distinctive corridor from
"Return of the Archons."

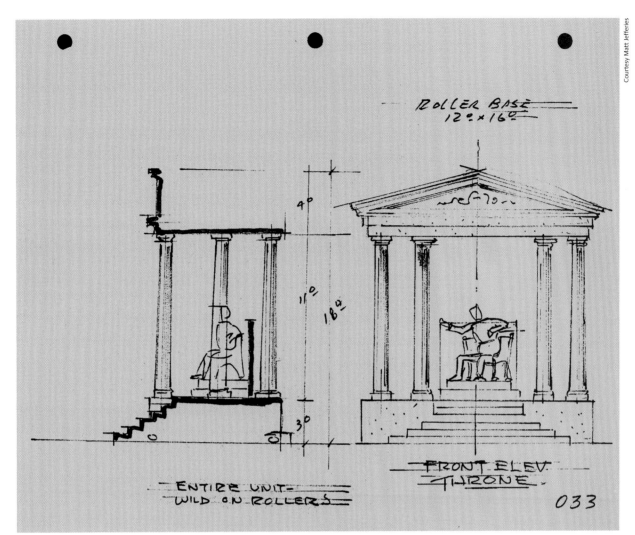

ROLLER BASE
12° × 16°

4°

11°

18°

3°

ENTIRE UNIT
WILD ON ROLLERS

FRONT ELEV.
THRONE.

033

47

"Who Mourns for Adonais?"
called for the creation of a
Greek temple set.

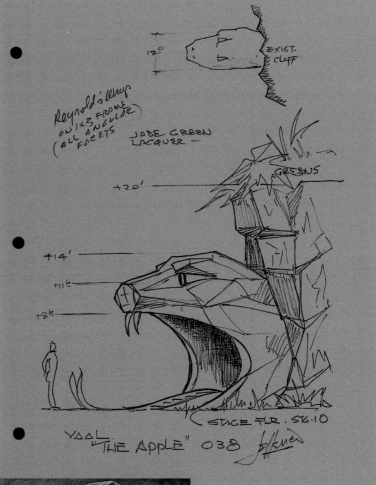

The computer/god Vaal, from "The Apple."

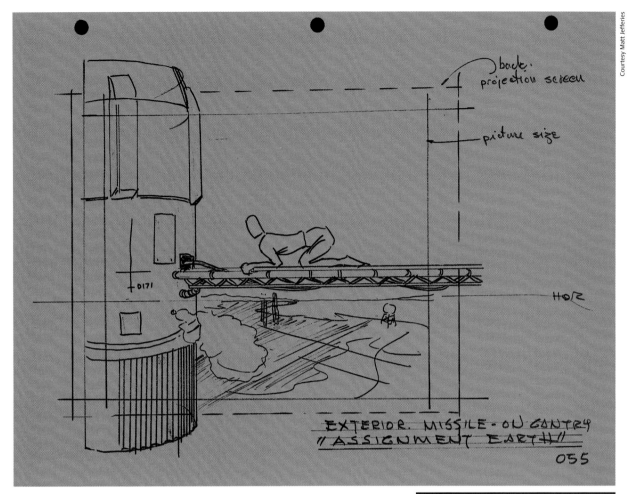

"Assignment: Earth" called for a close-up or a missile as part of Gary Seven's (Robert Lansing) assignment.

The creation of a new computer system for "Assignment: Earth"—one so advanced that even Spock (Leonard Nimoy) could not easily master it.

COMPUTER/SWINGING BOOKCASE
"ASSIGNMENT EARTH"
055

LIMBO-SALOON
"THE LAST GUNFIGHT"
056

The surreal exterior of
the saloon set from
"The Spectre of the Gun."

EXT. OBELISK

"PALEFACE"
60043-058

Courtesy Matt Jefferies

The obelisk from "Paradise Syndrome"; the episode's working title was "Paleface."

Paramount Pictures

A detail of the control
device from "Spock's Brain."

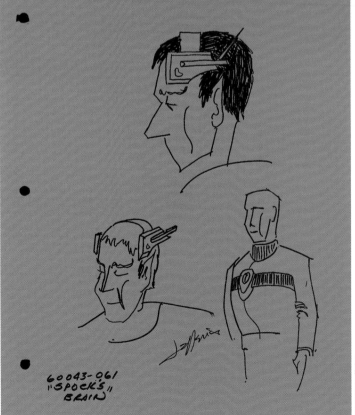

60043-061
"SPOCK'S"
BRAIN

53

From "Is There in
Truth No Beauty?":
the ambassador's habitat.

Finish as bronze —
Remote operate lid —
3 color internal floods
lite on cue.

Greens
high lites
on
bronze

AMBASSADOR'S
HABITAT
-062

54

Commander Spock escorts
the ambassador, in his
habitat, to his quarters.

Stratos, the cloud city from
"The Cloud Minders."

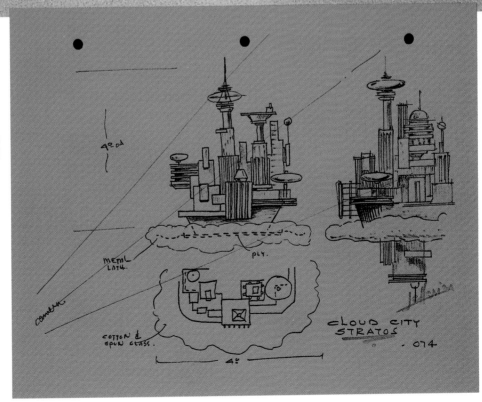

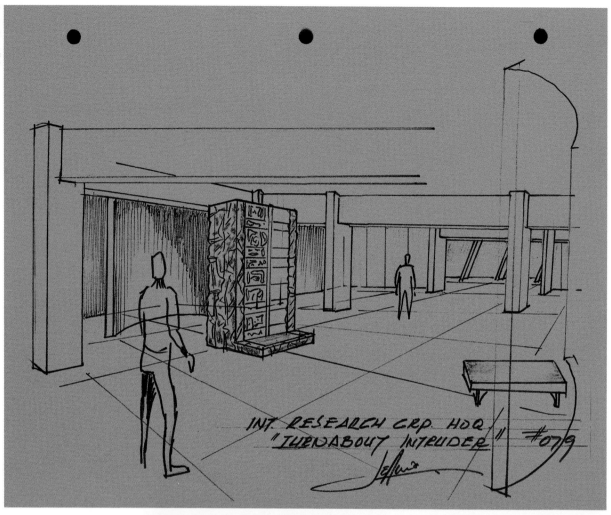

The machinery created for
the life-transference device
in "Turnabout Intruder."

In addition to the thousands of sketches created for projected scenes in Star Trek, whether or not they were used, Matt's collection includes a number of other sketches——mostly vehicles which were prepared for scenes that never aired, aliens that were never born, events that never happened, or sometimes just daydreams that remained in Matt's head. A few of these are depicted below for the pleasure of other dreamers.

REDRAW
ON
BLACK
MATTE BOARD
IN WHITE.

OBSOLETE
TRAMP FREIGHTER

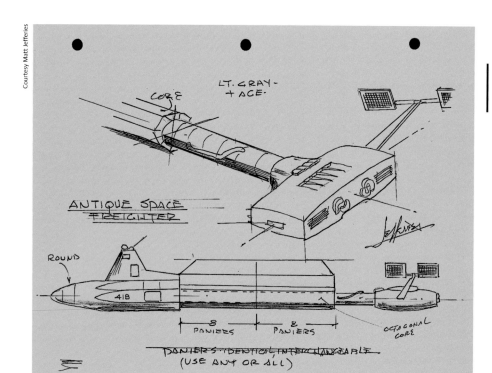

Labeled "antique space freighter," this ship became Khan's *Botany Bay* in "Space Seed."

Space dock/utility craft.

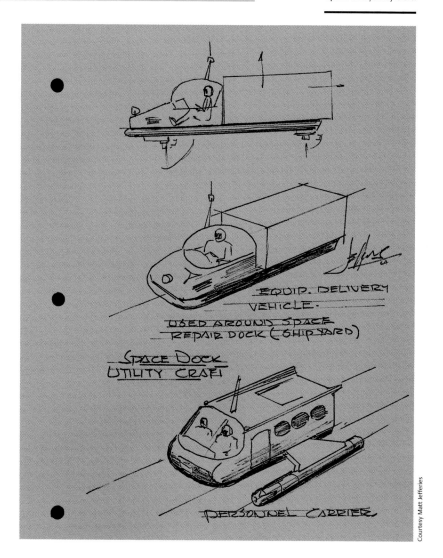

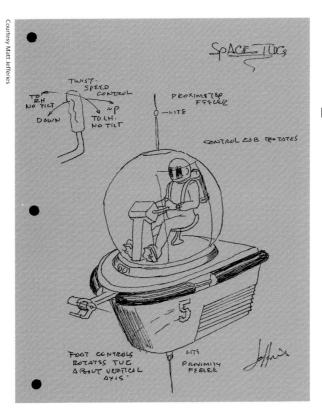

Space tug/service vehicle.

Space tug/service vehicle.

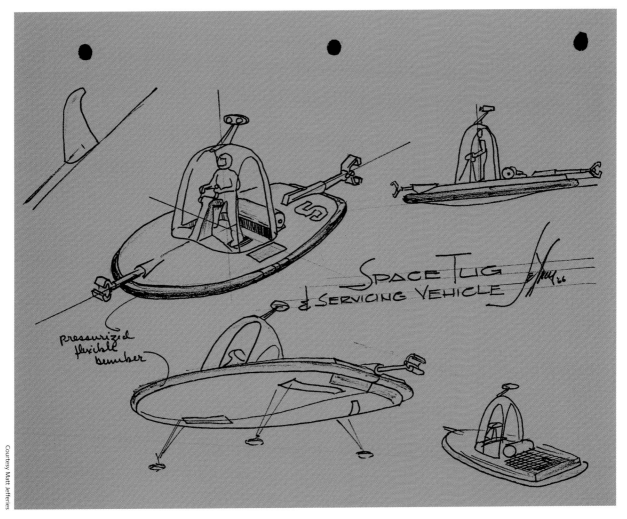

remove
bumper

TUG
SPACE, Co

61

Matt Jefferies, Part Two

The Search for the Enterprise

E X T E R I O R

The theory that space could be warped was first proposed by Albert Einstein in 1905, and first demonstrated, according to *Star Trek* canon, by Zefram Cochrane in 2063, proving that objects could travel faster than the speed of light. Warp drive is a delicately balanced, intricate web of chemistry, physics, mathematics, and mystery.

Matt Jefferies: "Outer space is probably the worst environment for a humanoid—even worse than being under the ocean. Without outside help, there's no way you can live. And since anything that man makes can break down, why put equipment outside the hull, where you'd have to go outside the ship to fix it? That—and my desire to play color off it—was the reason I kept the *Enterprise* exterior as plain as possible."

The ever-present hallmark of *Star Trek* is its dedication to fact within fiction— a practice never more explicitly applied than in the conception, design, and realization of the *Starship Enterprise*.

"It hadn't been decided what the serial number was going to be," Matt recalls, "so I gave the *Enterprise* my own designation, without any profound single reason for the sequence.

"Since the 1920's, N has indicated the United States in Navy terms, and C means 'commercial' vessel. I added an extra C just for fun. Interestingly, Russia's designation is CCC. So the N and the C together made it kind of international. After that, I had to pick some numbers. They had to be easily identifiable from a distance, so that eliminated 3, 8, 6, 9, and 4—none of which is that clear from a distance. That didn't leave much! So 1701 was as good a choice as any. The reason we gave for the choice afterwards was that the *Enterprise* was the 17th major design of the Federation, and the first in the series. 17 - 01!

"I was concerned about the design of a ship that Gene told me would have 'warp' drive. I thought, 'What the hell is warp drive?' But I gathered that this ship had to have powerful engines— extremely powerful. To me, that meant that they had to be designed away from the body. Boy, I tried a lot of

ideas. I wanted to stay away from the 'flying saucer' shape. The ball or sphere, as you'll see in some of the sketches, was my idea, but I ended up with the saucer after all. Gene would come in to look over what I was doing and say, 'I don't like this,' or, 'This looks good.' If Gene liked it, he'd ask the Boss [Herb Solow] and if the Boss liked it, then I'd work on that idea for a while.

"What I did do was to go out and buy everything I could get my hands on about Buck Rogers and Flash Gordon and so on. And of course, I was a member of the Aviation Space Writers' Association, so I had material that had come out of NASA and Northrop and Douglas and all the companies that had anything to do with space, and I pinned all that stuff up on one wall and said, 'That is what I will not do.' The negative/positive approach!

"So I worked on it for a while, and a couple of weeks later Herb and Gene came in. They liked a bit of this and a bit of that, and I worked on those bits. And then I came up with something I really liked, so I preloaded it—used lots of color and put it in a prominent place that made it kind of stand out. And that worked! It looked better than the other sketches and Gene said, 'That one looks good!' They [Herb and Gene]—and Bobby Justman, too, when he came aboard later—were a dream to work with."

BELOW ARE SOME OF THE SKETCHES MATT MADE TO DESIGN
THE SHIP THAT WOULD WARP SPACE AND TRAVEL TO THE STARS,
THE U.S.S. ENTERPRISE, NCC-1701.

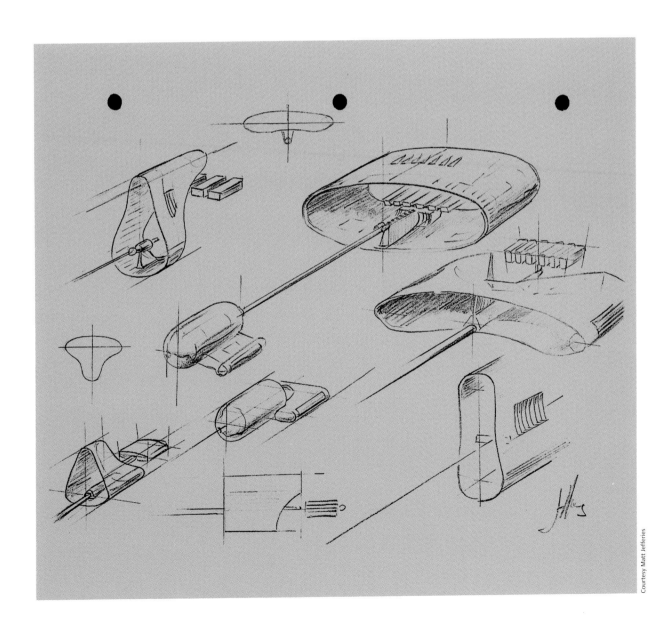

63

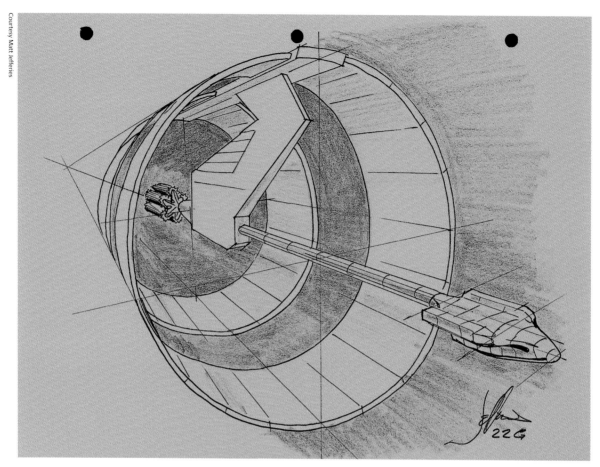

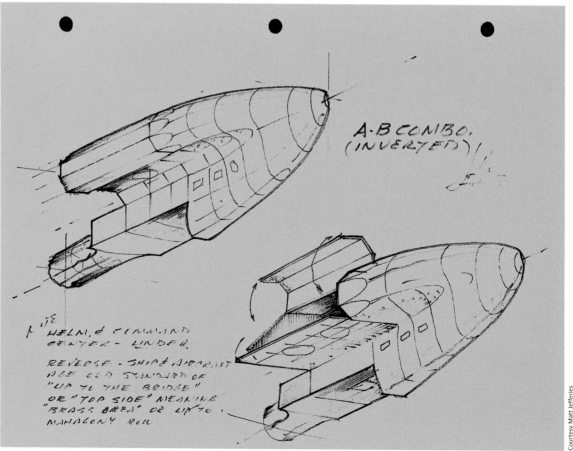

A·B COMBO.
(INVERTED)

HELM, & COMMAND
CENTER - UNDER.

REVERSE - SHIP & AIRCRAFT
AGE OLD STANDARD OF
"UP TO THE BRIDGE"
OR "TOP SIDE" MEANING
"BRASS AREA" OR LIFT TO
MAHAGONY ROW

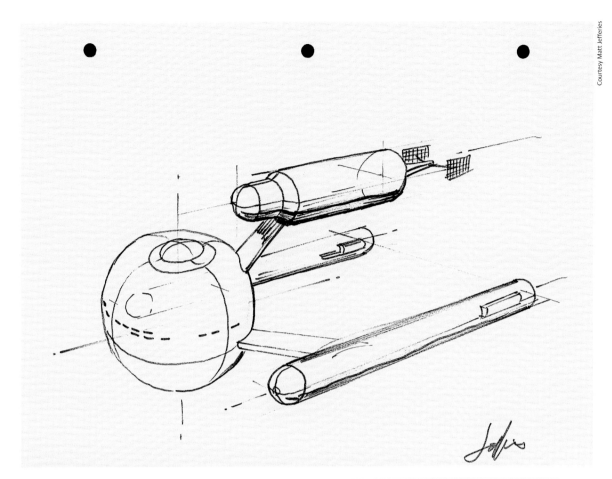

65

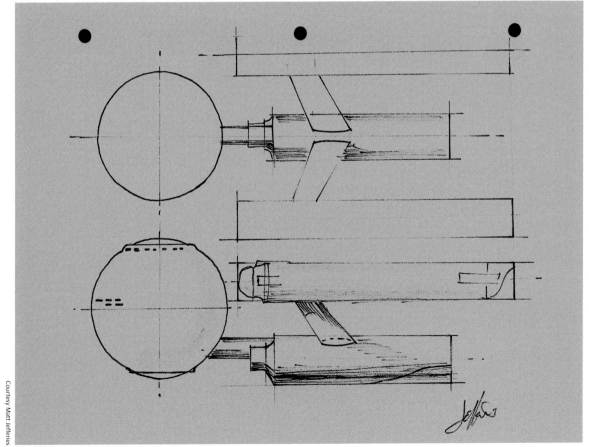

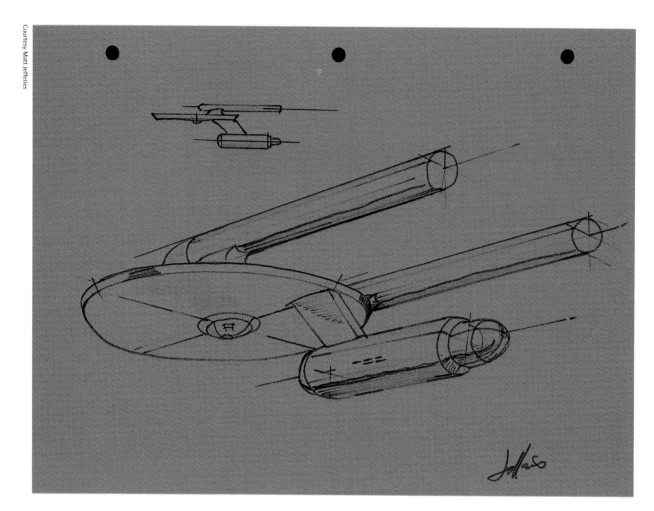

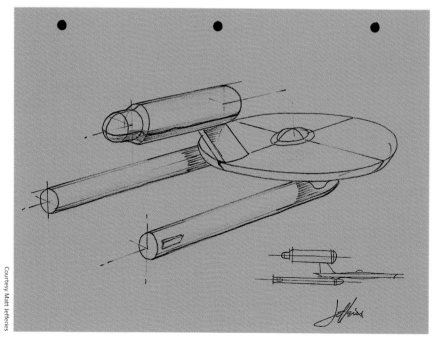

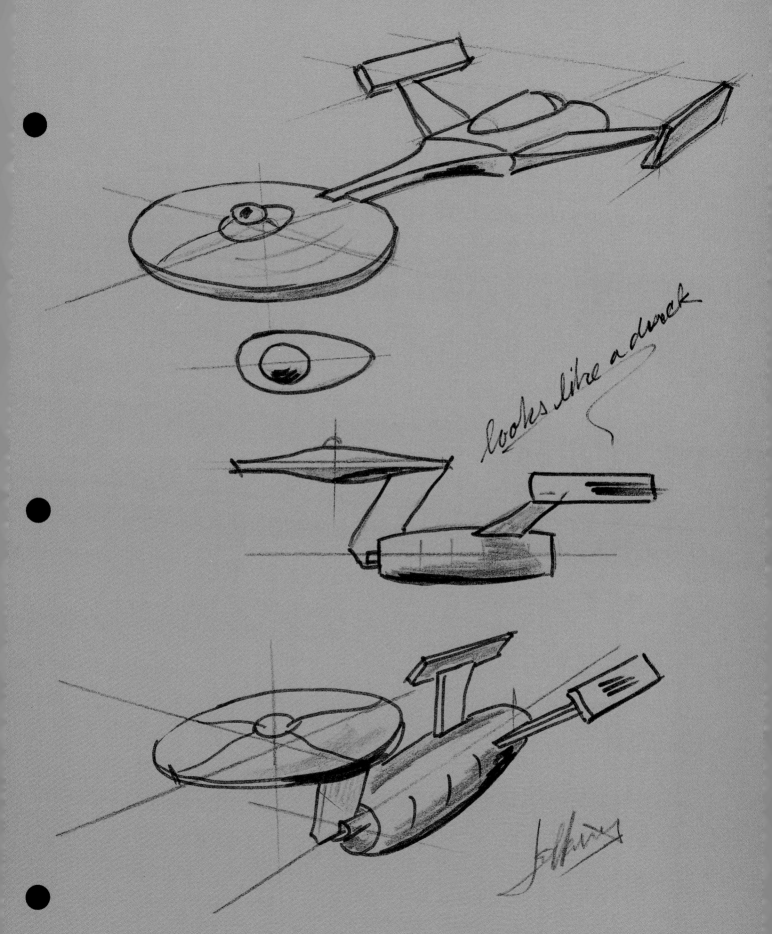

looks like a duck

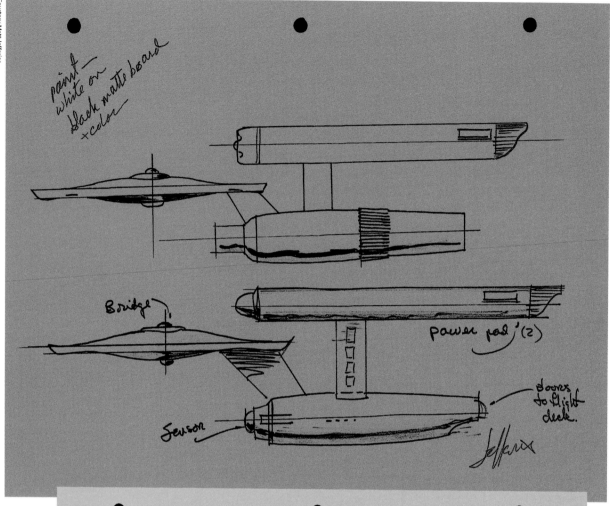

paint —
white on
black matte board
+color

Bridge

Sensor

power pad's (2)

doors
to flight
deck.

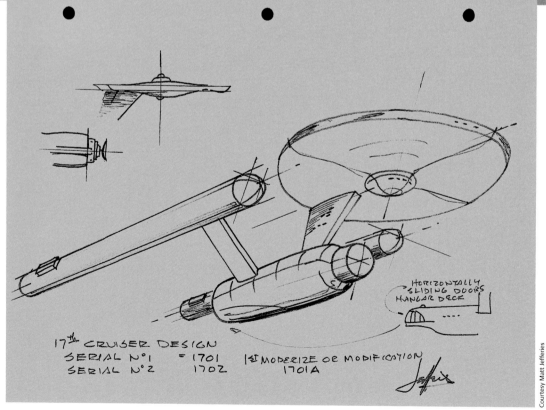

HORIZONTALLY
SLIDING DOORS
HANGAR DECK

17th CRUISER DESIGN
SERIAL N°1   = 1701   1st MODERIZE OR MODIFICATION
SERIAL N°2   1702   1701A

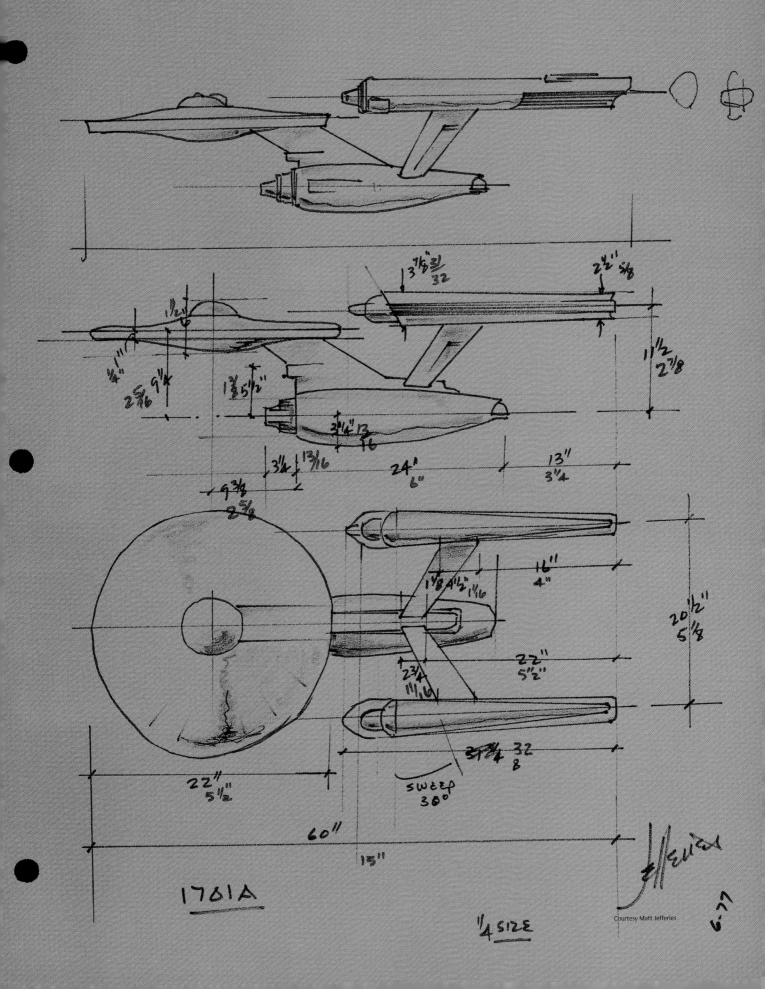

3⅞" 3¾/32

2½" 5/8

1½"/2
1½/2
2⅞

¼"/4
2⅝/16 9"/4

1¾/8 5½"/2

2¼"/4 13/16

3½"/4 13/16

24"/6"

13"/3¾

9¾/8
2⅝/8

1⅛/8 4½"/2 1½/16

16"/4"

20½"/5⅛

2¾/4 11/16

22"/5½"

22"/5½"

3¾/4 32/8

1701A

¼ SIZE

Courtesy Matt Jefferies

6-77

WHEN THE FINAL SKETCH HAD BEEN

APPROVED, MATT MADE A FEW ADDITIONAL

REFINEMENTS BEFORE THE SPECIFICATIONS

WENT TO THE MODEL MAKER.

THE FINAL DRAWING, WHICH WOULD BE USED

FOR THE THREE-DIMENSIONAL MODEL, WAS

FOUND AMONG MATT JEFFERIES'S FILES,

LABELED SIMPLY "SKETCH 300: 3-VIEW

SCALE ANNOTATED.

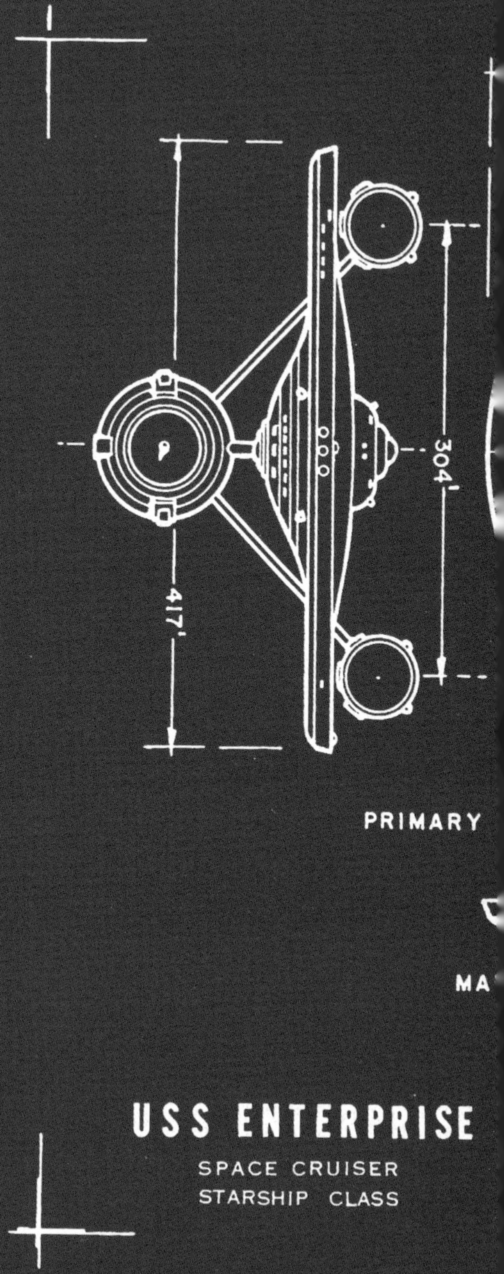

304'

417'

PRIMARY

MA

USS ENTERPRISE
SPACE CRUISER
STARSHIP CLASS

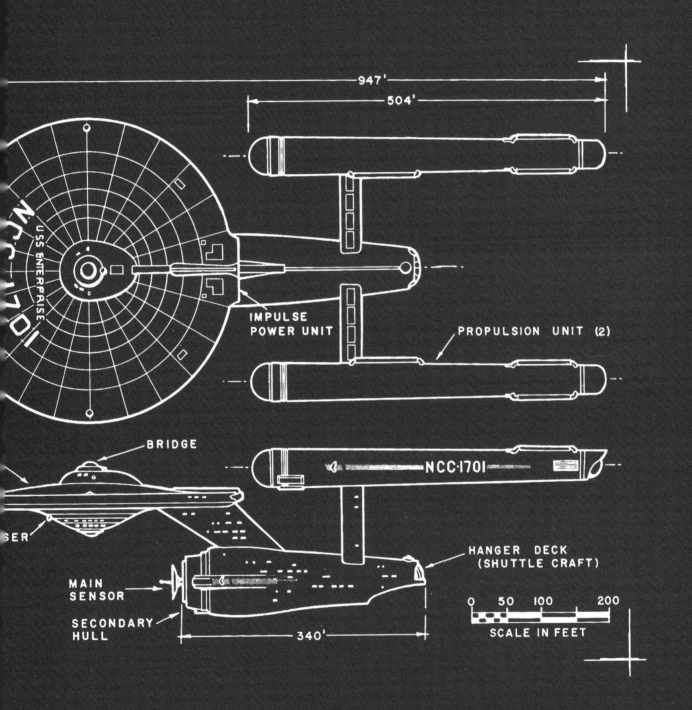

947'

504'

IMPULSE
POWER UNIT

PROPULSION UNIT (2)

U.S.S. ENTERPRISE

NCC-1701

BRIDGE

SER

MAIN
SENSOR

SECONDARY
HULL

HANGER DECK
(SHUTTLE CRAFT)

340'

0   50   100   200
SCALE IN FEET

71

Courtesy Matt Jefferies

Matt Jefferies, Part Two

The Search for the Enterprise

I N T E R I O R

"My big problem," Matt remembers, "was coming up with ideas that you could do on time with the available resources. Great ideas sometimes need great amounts of money and a lot of time to execute. We needed a space, for example, where Scotty could fix things without taking up too much room. So I made a tube with all kinds of complicated-looking stuff in it, and it worked, I guess. Somebody hung the name Jefferies Tube on it. It wasn't me, but the name stuck and I used it in some of my sketches!"

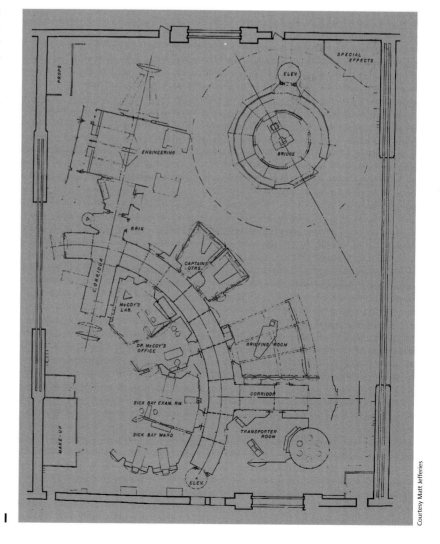

Enterprise interior sets, stage plan. ▌

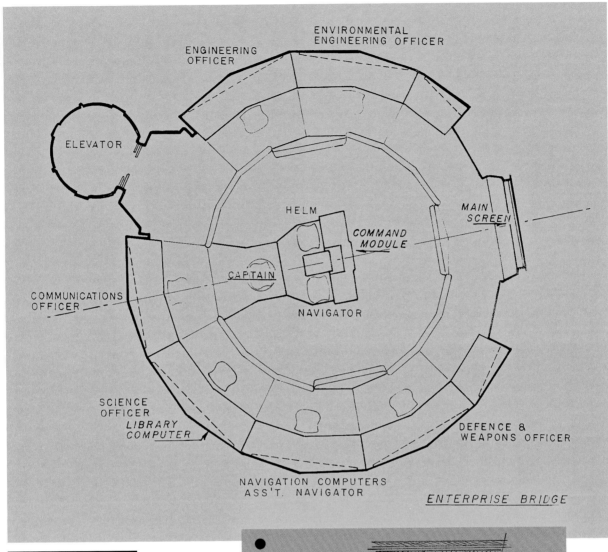

Courtesy Matt Jefferies

ENVIRONMENTAL
ENGINEERING OFFICER

ENGINEERING
OFFICER

ELEVATOR

HELM

COMMAND
MODULE

MAIN
SCREEN

CAPTAIN

NAVIGATOR

COMMUNICATIONS
OFFICER

SCIENCE
OFFICER
*LIBRARY
COMPUTER*

DEFENCE &
WEAPONS OFFICER

NAVIGATION COMPUTERS
ASS'T. NAVIGATOR

ENTERPRISE BRIDGE

Enterprise bridge annotated plan.

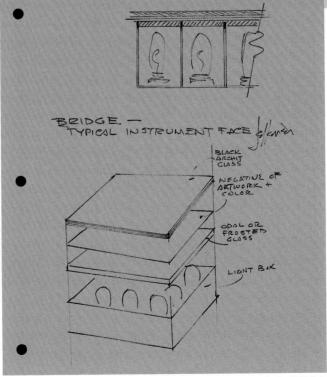

BRIDGE. —
TYPICAL INSTRUMENT FACE

BLACK
ARCHIT
GLASS

NEGATIVE OF
ARTWORK +
COLOR

OPAL OR
FROSTED
GLASS

LIGHT BOX

Typical bridge instrument.

Courtesy Matt Jefferies

73

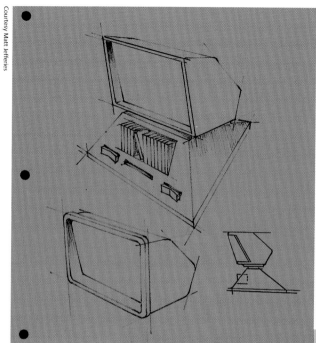

Viewing screens—various.

Instrument consoles—wild units. Wild units
are sections of a set made to be removable,
in order to accommodate camera placement.

WILD CONSOLES

ADD:
ACCESS PANELS -
FOR REPAIR SCENES.
LITE EFFECTS
MURPHY'S LOW.

74

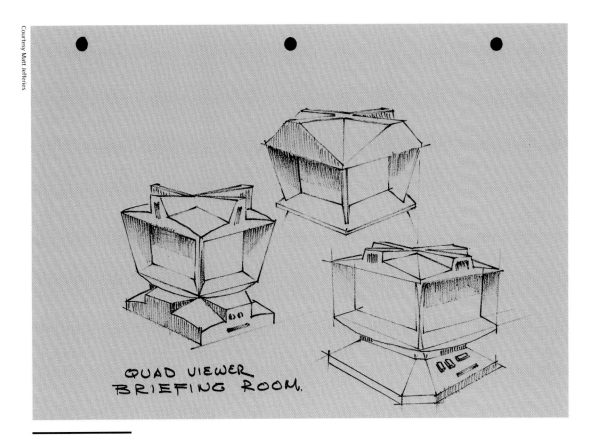

QUAD VIEWER
BRIEFING ROOM.

Viewing screens—various.

Corridor, *Enterprise* interior.

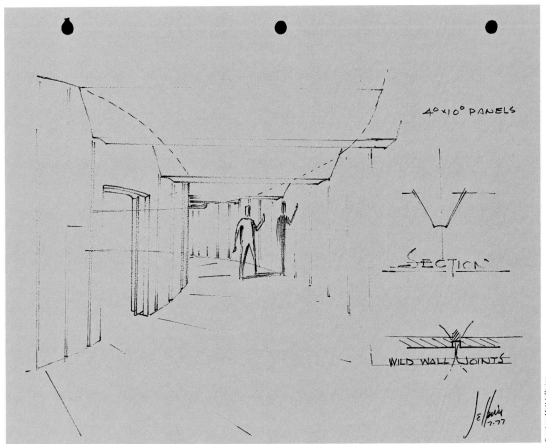

4°×10° PANELS

SECTION

WILD WALL JOINTS

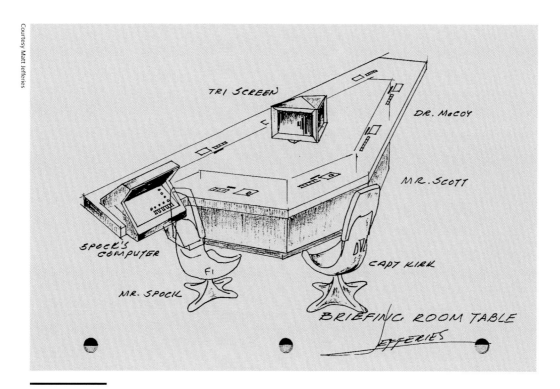

Briefing room table.

Sickbay, examination room.

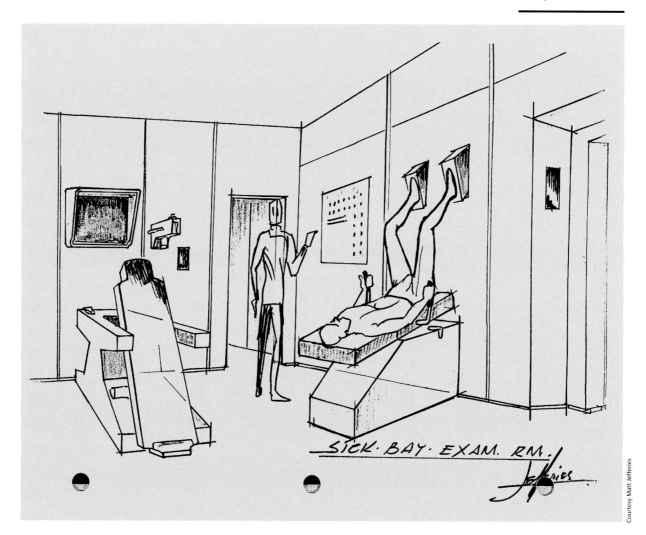

CAPT. KIRK'S QTRS.

Kirk's quarters.

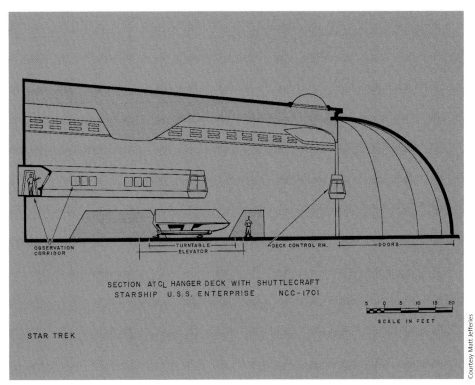

OBSERVATION
CORRIDOR

TURNTABLE
ELEVATOR

DECK CONTROL RM.

DOORS

SECTION AT CL HANGER DECK WITH SHUTTLECRAFT
STARSHIP U.S.S. ENTERPRISE   NCC-1701

5 0 5 10 15 20

SCALE IN FEET

STAR TREK

Enterprise hangar deck,
interior side view.

The Search for the Klingon Cruiser

Star Trek producer-writer Gene Coon created the Klingon race. Matt Jefferies created their vessel. Matt remembers his efforts on the Klingon design: "I designed the Klingon ship at home—there was just too much going on at the studio from morning till night. Since the Klingons were the enemy, I had to design a ship that would be instantly recognizable as an enemy ship, especially for a flash cut. There had to be no way it could be mistaken for our guys. It had to look threatening, even vicious. So I modeled it on a manta ray, both shape and color, and that's why it looks as it does in the original series."

Courtesy Matt Jefferies

MATT JEFFERIES WAS "NEVER A SCIENCE-FICTION GUY," AS HE PUTS IT.
BUT SINCE HE WAS A DEDICATED PILOT, HIS APPROACH TO THE DESIGN OF
THE KLINGON CRUISER WAS AERODYNAMIC.

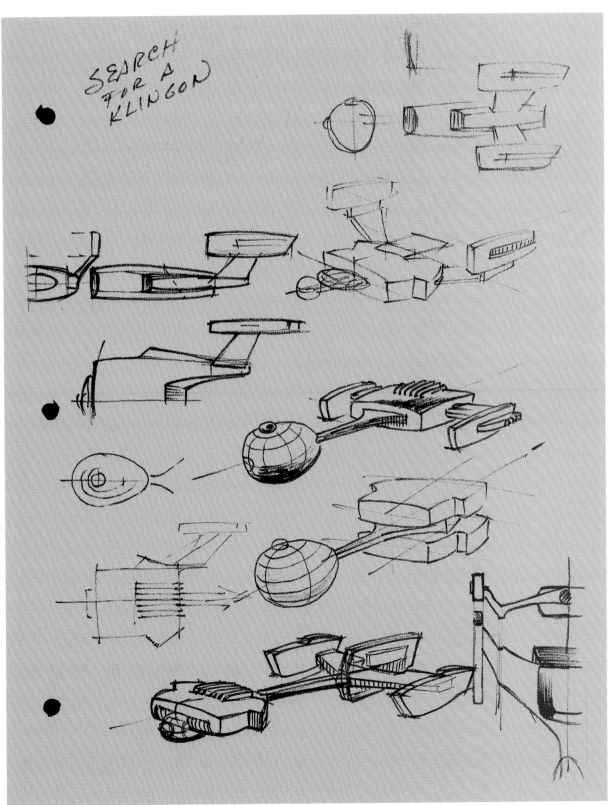

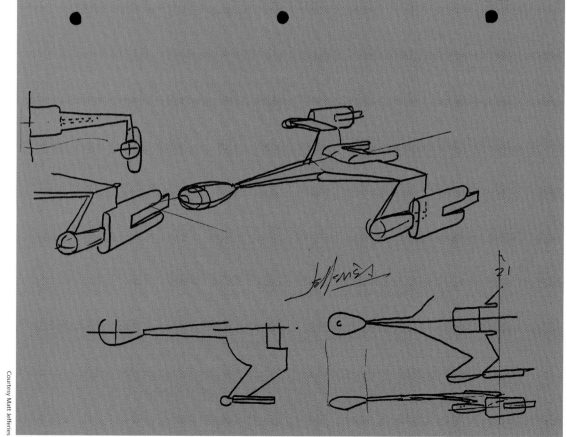

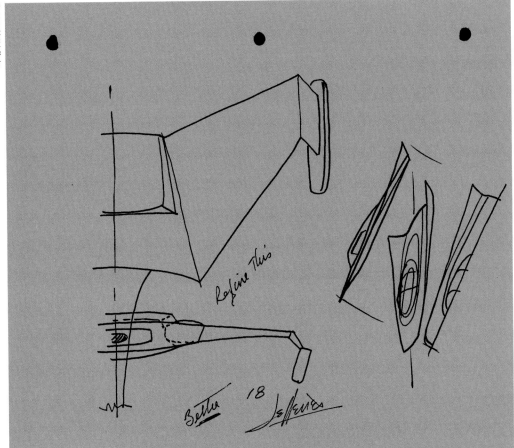

Refine this

Better 18 Jefferies

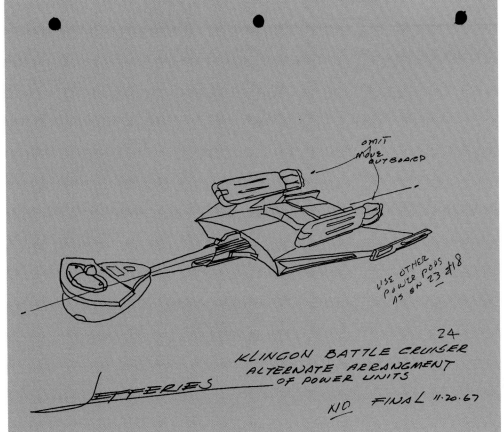

OMIT
MOVE
OUTBOARD

USE OTHER
POWER PODS
AS ON 23 #18

24

JEFFERIES

KLINGON BATTLE CRUISER
ALTERNATE ARRANGMENT
OF POWER UNITS

NO FINAL 11-20-67

FULL SIZE FOR TOOLING
MINATURE

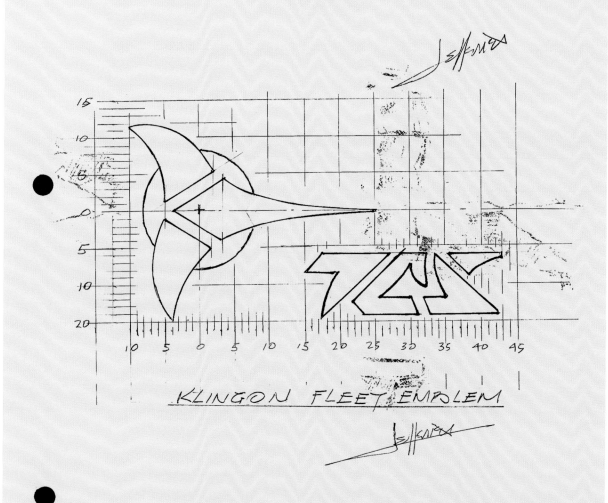

KLINGON FLEET EMBLEM

82

Matt also designed the
Klingon Fleet emblem.

"THE THREE-DIMENSIONAL MODEL WE USED WAS BASED ON MY FINAL SKETCH," MATT RECALLS. "IT WAS SENT TO AMT [AMERICAN MODEL TOY CORPORATION], AND THEY RETURNED A MASTER TOOLING MODEL WHICH WE USED IN THE SHOW. THAT MODEL WAS GIVEN TO THE NATIONAL AIR AND SPACE MUSEUM MANY YEARS AGO. I'M ASSUMING IT'S STILL THERE, ALONG WITH THE ENTERPRISE."

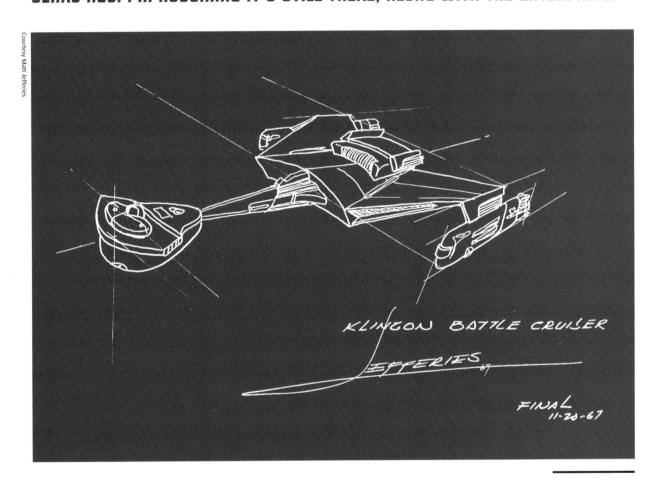

Final design for the Klingon battle cruiser.

Master tooling model of Klingon ship.

The model for the *Constitution*-class *Enterprise* and the Klingon battle cruiser are part of the permanent collection of the Smithsonian's Air and Space Museum.

Matt Jefferies, Part Four

Scale Drawings Comparisons

EVER THOROUGH, MATT MADE SEVERAL SKETCHES COMPARING THE SIZE AND DESIGN OF THE ENTERPRISE, THE KLINGON CRUISER, AND A UNITED STATES NAVY AIRCRAFT CARRIER. HIS KNOWLEDGE OF SHIP AND AIRCRAFT ENGINEERING AND DESIGN IN THE REAL WORLD WAS AN INVALUABLE ASSET IN RENDERING THE PRECISE CALCULATIONS NEEDED TO ACCOMMODATE PERSONNEL AND EQUIPMENT ON THE IMAGINARY SHIPS.

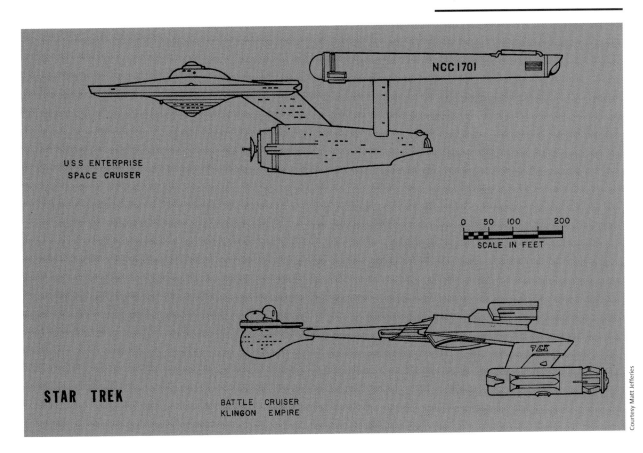

STARSHIP U.S.S. ENTERPRISE (BLACK)   U.S. NAVY AIRCRAFT CARRIER CVA-65 ENTERPRISE (GRAY)

HANGER DECK
(SHUTTLE CRAFT)

0   50   100   200
SCALE IN FEET

STAR TREK
STARSHIP ENTERPRISE

Starship Enterprise and U.S. Navy aircraft carrier—comparison scale plans.

Enterprise to Klingon size comparison—side view.

U S S ENTERPRISE
SPACE CRUISER

NCC 1701

0   50   100   200
SCALE IN FEET

STAR TREK

BATTLE   CRUISER
KLINGON EMPIRE

Shuttlecraft

Shuttlecraft have been an important means of transportation in every incarnation of *Star Trek*. Most shuttlecraft are named for famous explorers or scientists, beginning with the original that Matt designed, the one that came to be known as the *Galileo*.

Matt's sketches, doodles, and scale drawings barely indicate the time-consuming process of arriving at the finished product; however, the drawings below were the only ones found.

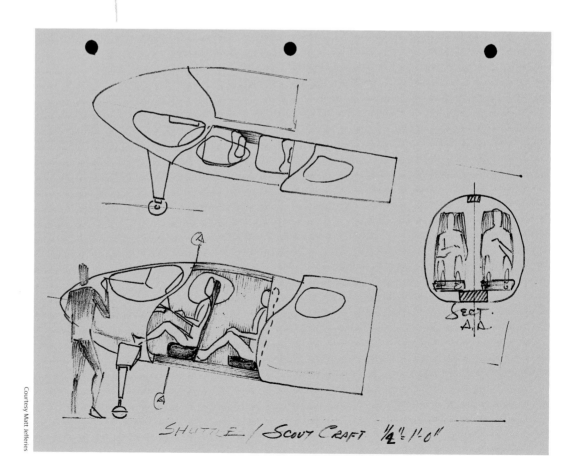

Courtesy Matt Jefferies

SHUTTLE / SCOUT CRAFT ¼" = 1'-0"

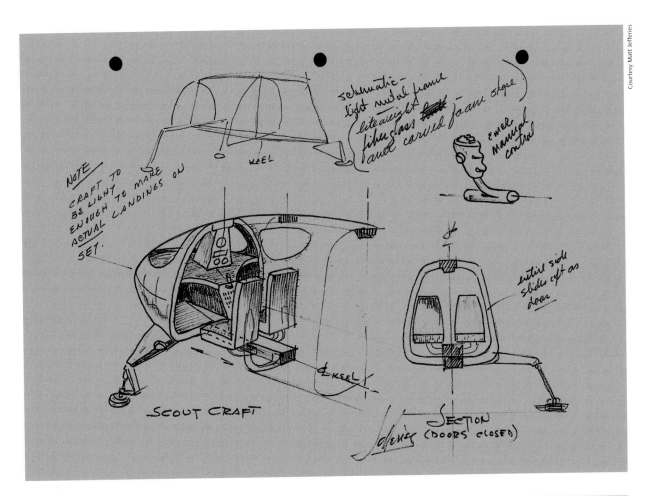

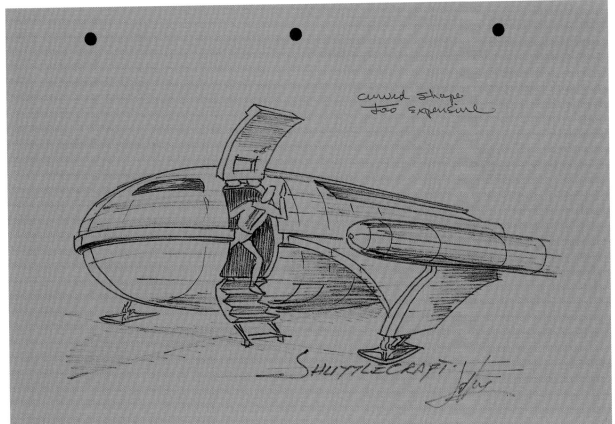

87

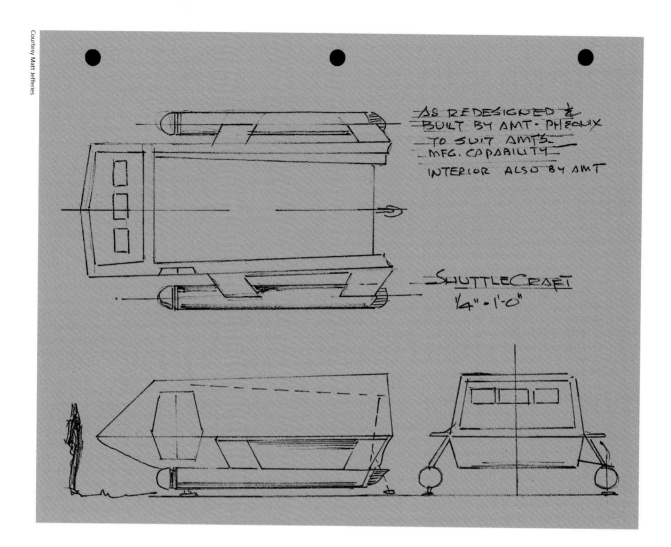

AS REDESIGNED &
BUILT BY AMT · PHEONIX
TO SUIT AMTS
MFG. CAPABILITY
INTERIOR ALSO BY AMT

SHUTTLECRAFT
¼" - 1'-0"

88

STAR TREK

SCALE IN FEET

SHUTTLECRAFT – LEFT SIDE

The final result of Matt's sketches
appeared to entice viewers to "tune in
next week" when *The Original Series* aired.

89

Weapons

MATT IS PARTICULARLY FOND OF THE FEDERATION HAND PHASER.
HE ALSO DESIGNED A NUMBER OF OTHER WEAPONS, AND PROPS
USED AS WEAPONS. AMONG THE ORIGINAL SKETCHES STILL IN HIS
COLLECTION, HOWEVER, ONLY A FEW WEAPON DRAWINGS REMAIN.

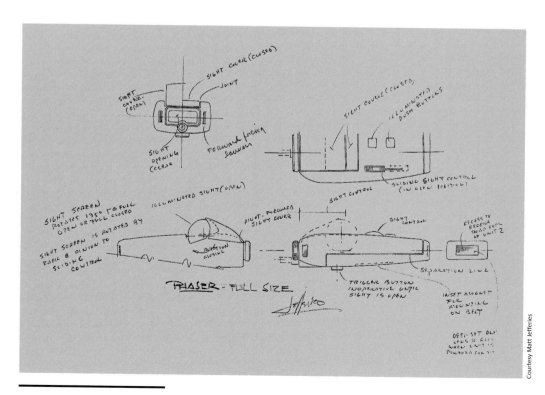

Courtesy Matt Jefferies

Phaser weapons, detail scale drawings.

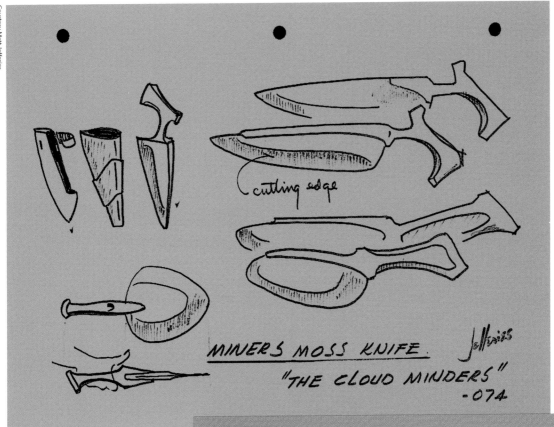

cutting edge

MINERS MOSS KNIFE.   Jefferies

"THE CLOUD MINDERS"
-074

The Troglyte weapon used in
"The Cloud Minders."

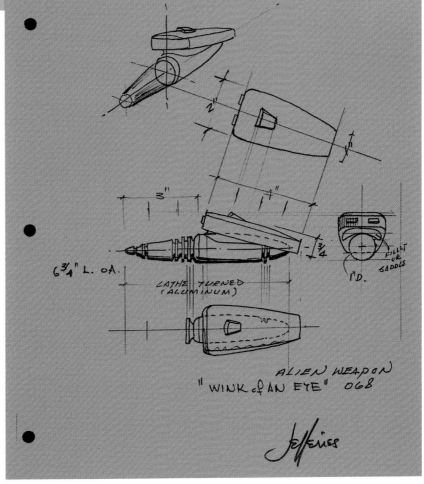

91

2"

3"   1"   4"

3/4"

6 3/4" L. OA.

LATHE TURNED
(ALUMINUM)

FILLET
OR
SADDLE

1"D.

ALIEN WEAPON
"WINK of AN EYE" 068

Jefferies

Scalosian weapon, from "Wink of an Eye."

Phaser weapons,
detail scale drawings.

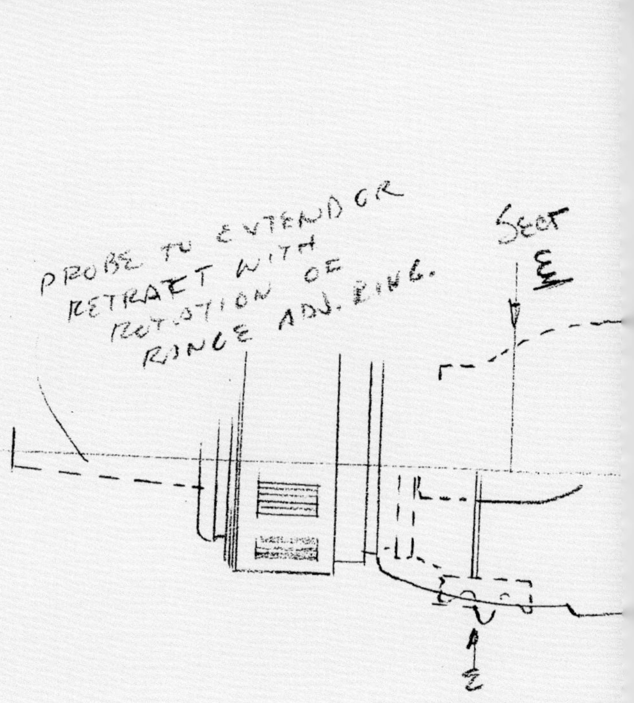
PROBE TO EXTEND OR RETRACT WITH ROTATION OF RANGE ADJ. RING.
SECT E
E

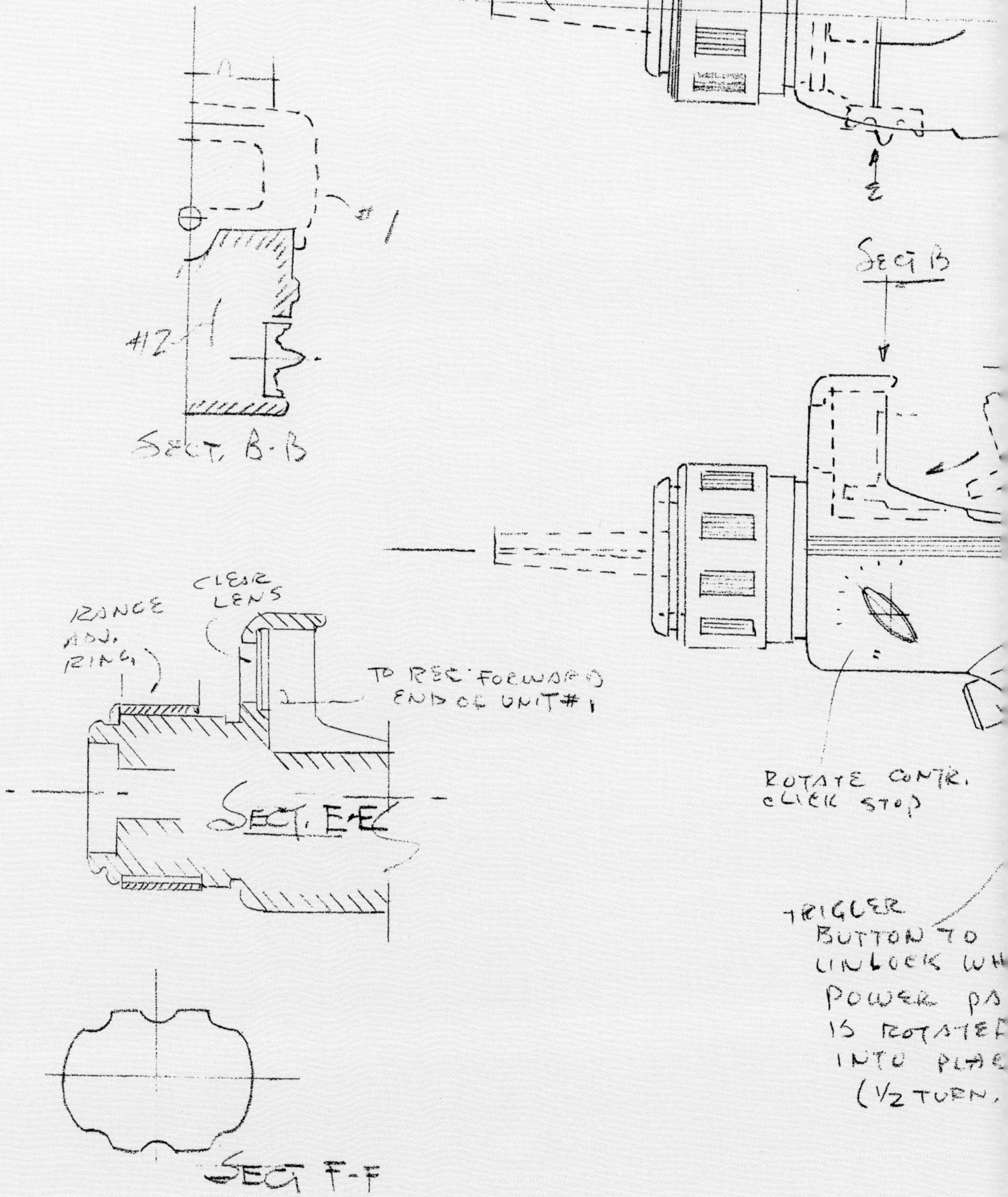
#1
#2
SECT. B-B
SECT B
RANGE ADJ. RING
CLEAR LENS
TO REC. FORWARD END OF UNIT #1
SECT. E-E
ROTATE CONTR. CLICK STOP
TRIGGER BUTTON TO UNLOCK WH
POWER PA
IS ROTATE
INTO PLAC
(1/2 TURN.
SECT F-F

Courtesy Matt Jefferies

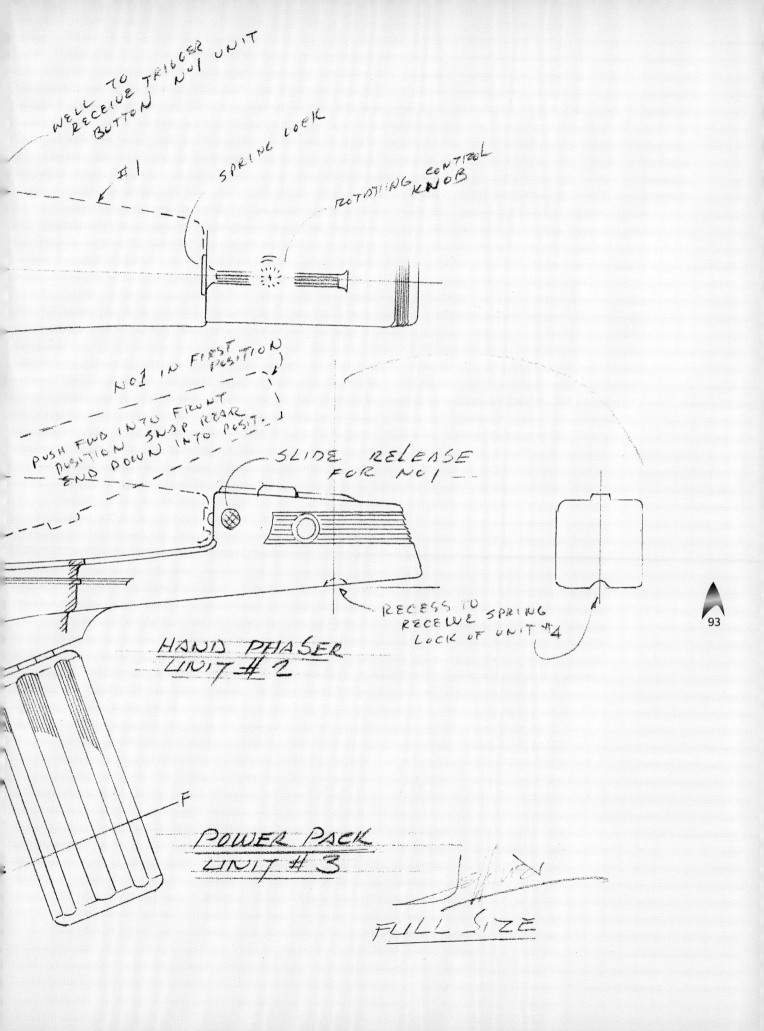

WELL TO RECEIVE TRIGGER
BUTTON NO1 UNIT

#1

SPRING LOCK

ROTATING CONTROL KNOB

NO1 IN FIRST POSITION

PUSH FWD INTO FRONT POSITION. SNAP REAR END DOWN INTO POSIT.

SLIDE RELEASE FOR NO1

RECESS TO RECEIVE SPRING LOCK OF UNIT #4

HAND PHASER
UNIT #2

F

POWER PACK
UNIT #3

FULL SIZE

Matt Jefferies, Part Seven

The Lost Set

As if Matt Jefferies didn't have enough problems physically designing the *Star Trek* series, a new and very immediate problem faced him in early May 1966. Each and every week thereafter, a *Star Trek* director would show up on his doorstep with a deceptively simple request: "I'm ready to go down to the stage to see the sets, so I can plan how to shoot my episode. Can you walk me through?" It was a question to which there was no readily available answer.

There was no way Matt could walk the directors through the sets, because each episode had its own set requirements and there just wasn't enough stage space available to keep all the permanent sets standing. There was no way Matt could tell the directors to screen the pilot, "Where No Man Has Gone Before," because so much had been changed when the sets were moved from the Desilu Culver studios, where the pilot had been shot, to the Desilu Gower studios, where the

series was being filmed. There was no way Matt could tell the directors to watch NBC at 8:30 on Thursday nights to get a look at the sets and get a feeling for the series—because *Star Trek* had not as yet premiered. But the always-resourceful Matt Jefferies had planned ahead. "Follow me," he'd say, "to another room here in the art department, and I'll show you!"

Matt had spent his weekends at home building, on his own time, with his own money and with his own materials, a four-foot by four-foot, three-dimensional scale model of Desilu Stage 9 to depict what all of *Star Trek*'s permanent sets would look like if they were ever put up at the same time. It hung from an art department wall and gave the directors the only practical, three-dimensional look at their permanent sets until that morning, seven to fourteen days hence, when they would show up on the real stage to direct *Star Trek*.

We spent many hours with Matt at his home office and workroom and at his airplane hangar and hangar/apartment. It was during one of those "at home" research sessions that Matt remembered the scale model he'd made over thirty years ago. So—into the recesses of his basement he went—and emerged triumphant, with the old model still intact.

Here is the "lost set" as every director of the *Star Trek* classic series saw it then.

Enterprise lost set.

EVERY STAR TREK *VIEWER WILL BE ABLE TO IDENTIFY THE VARIOUS COMPONENTS OF THE U.S.S. ENTERPRISE. HOWEVER, THIS MODEL, HAVING BEEN MADE FOR THE DIRECTORS, DEMONSTRATES THE RELATIONSHIP AMONG THE VARIOUS SETS. ANY VISITOR TO DESILU STAGE 9 DURING THE FILMING OF THE ORIGINAL SERIES WOULD HAVE SEEN THE SHIP IN THIS LAYOUT. WITHIN THE FICTIONAL WORLD, OF COURSE, ENGINEERING WOULD BE ON A DIFFERENT LEVEL FROM THE BRIDGE.*

The view from the transporter room.

Looking across sickbay.

Looking down on sickbay, a director
would see how the rooms related.

99

A "ground level" view showing the
hallway and the transporter console.

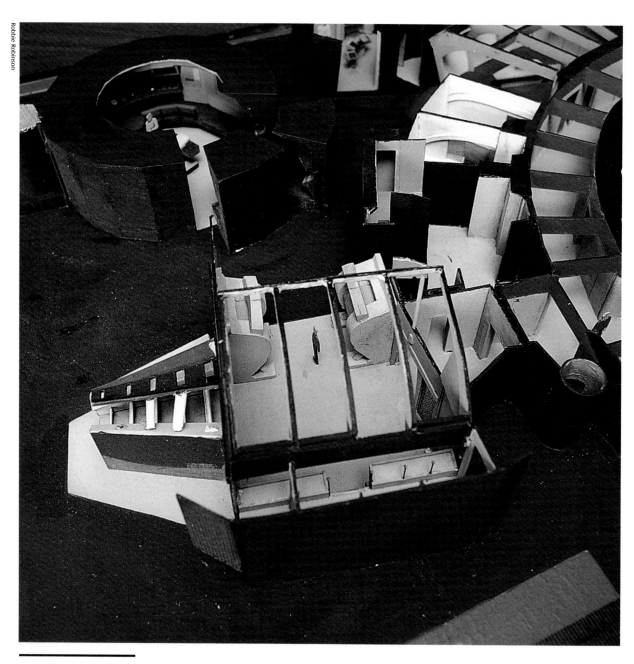

Looking down on engineering.

101

The rarely seen auxiliary control room.

The corridors of the *Enterprise*.

103

This overview shows the
advantage of the curved corridor.

An overview of the bridge.

A close-up of auxiliary control.

Sickbay's examination room.

107

Close-up of the corridor,
showing the overhangs.

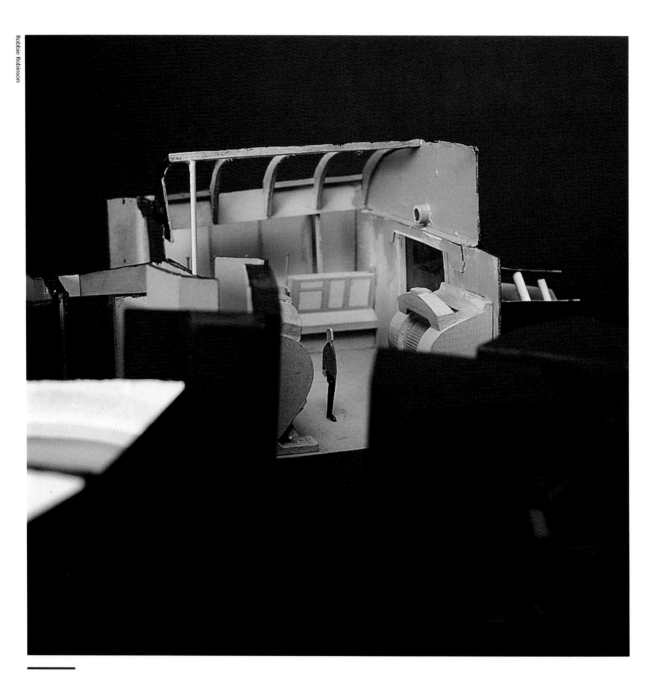

Engineering.

109

Next to the secondary engineering
control room is the "crew quarters" set.

A "ground-level" view shows how the sets
were constructed to fit in the saucer section.

111

A reverse view of the lost set.

A close-up of auxiliary control,
conveniently next to the bridge.

The following photograph is not from the lost set, but is, rather, the hull-pressure indicator screen from the set of the original bridge of the *Enterprise*. It was removed during the shooting of "Day of the Dove" and was taken to an insert stage to be filmed. After its use on the insert stage, the screen was returned to Matt's office and placed on his desk amongst piles of miscellaneous odds and ends. As sometimes happens during the rush of production, the screen, designed and constructed by Matt, never made its way back to the bridge. The series continued shooting without it.

WHEN WE UNCOVERED THE LOST SET, WE ALSO FOUND THIS SET PIECE.

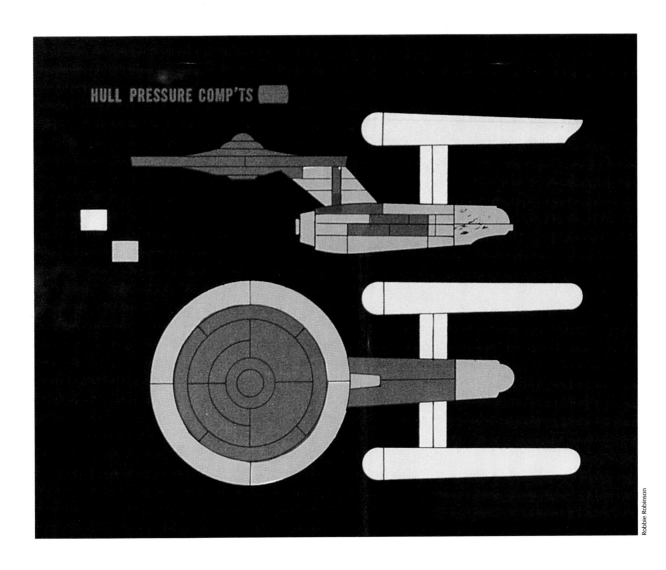

HULL PRESSURE COMP'TS

Matt Jefferies, Art Director

"When I started on *Star Trek*," Matt remembers, "Gene didn't even have an office, much less a secretary. Only Herb was on the lot. But Gene came to the lot most days, and at first I dealt directly with him. Then the studio brought in a man by the name of Franz Bachelin, an old-time art director. They also brought in a friend of Desi [Arnaz], Art Director Pato Guzman from *The Lucy Show*. Bachelin and Guzman were to be art directors number one and number two on *Star Trek*. I was still a set designer, not an art director. I would

114

have the bridge and the exterior of the ship to do and they were to do the rest. After the first pilot, they both bailed out. I became an acting art director and did the second pilot. After that, I did the pilot for *Mission: Impossible* and then a lovely little western called *The Long Hunt of April Savage*. Herb Solow was in charge of both of those. Then I was loaned to Disney to do a set for one of their movies, after which I returned to *Star Trek*.

"There were problems in becoming an 'official' art director. The application was put in to the union and I waited. A good friend of mine who was on the executive board told me what was happening. When my acceptance came up at a meeting, the president said, 'Well, we'll table that for the time being, until the series [*Star Trek*] is canceled—there's no way it will get renewed. Matt won't be working, and if Matt isn't working, that will take care of the problem and we can forget him.'

"Well, I went and told Gene about it. Gene called Herb. Herb called me over and told me, 'You're going to be working here, and you'll be working here as an art director until you are approved and sworn in, even if we have to keep you sweeping the stages to do it!' Well, thanks to Herb, I stayed. It finally got sorted out, and I got my official credit, sometime after the first season of *Star Trek*."

DIRECTOR OF PHOTOGRAPHY
ERNEST HALLER, A.S.C.

PRODUCTION DESIGNER
WALTER M. JEFFERIES

Matt Jefferies's unofficial production designer credit.

Matt's official art director credit.

ART DIRECTOR
WALTER M. JEFFERIES

DIRECTOR OF PHOTOGRAPHY
AL FRANCIS

115

WILLIAM WARE THEISS

The career of William Ware Theiss—he used his middle name to differentiate himself from a New York clothes designer named William Theiss—as a wardrobe man and costume designer in the motion picture and television industries spanned over thirty years. In various capacities, he assisted in the design of costumes and/or fully designed costumes for over seventeen feature motion pictures.

The first major film on which Bill Theiss worked was *Spartacus*. He was one of many wardrobe people to contribute to director Stanley Kubrick's star-studded spectacular. Bill then dressed Peter Sellers in Blake Edwards's *The Pink Panther*. After his work on *Star Trek*, Theiss was hired by Herb Solow, then Vice President of Worldwide Production for MGM, to work on *Pretty Maids All in a Row*. The producer for the film was Gene Roddenberry.

Hal Ashby's black comedy, *Harold and Maude* (1971), featured memorable performances by Bud Cort, Ruth Gordon, and Vivian Pickles, and the costuming of Bill Theiss. *Bound For Glory* (1976), also directed by Ashby, told the story of American folksinger and political activist Woody Guthrie. It won an Academy Award nomination for Theiss, for his authentic 1930's Great Depression working-class costumes.

Bill worked for the Walt Disney Company on *Pete's Dragon* (1977). Half of the characters were animated, so Bill only dressed the eclectic group of "live" actors. Bill also worked on *Goin' South* (1978), *Children of Sanchez* (1978), *Who'll Stop the Rain* (1978), and *Butch and Sundance: The Early Years* (1979).

It was unexpected that this last film, a retrospective conception of the early years before the original, *Butch Cassidy and the Sundance Kid*, would gain attention from the members of the Academy of Motion Picture Arts and Sciences. It did, but only for Bill Theiss. He was nominated for an Academy Award for Outstanding Costume Design.

In 1983, Bill Theiss was again nominated for an Academy Award, for his design of "funny car" clothes for *Heart Like a Wheel*.

Although Bill Theiss personally received Academy Award nominations for three of his films—*Bound For Glory* in 1976, *Butch and Sundance: The Early Years* in 1979, and *Heart Like a Wheel* in 1983—he never won an Oscar. But receiving a nomination singled him out as one of that year's five best motion-picture costume designers—out of the hundreds of motion-picture costume designers, both in Hollywood and in other motion-picture production centers around the world.

Bill Theiss is best remembered as the designer of every costume worn in the 79 episodes that comprise the first *Star Trek* series. From Captain Kirk's tunic, to Edith Keeler's dowdy dress, to the now-infamous daring attire of almost all other female guest stars, Bill dressed them all.

Very little is publicly known about Bill Theiss, who died in 1992. He was a solitary man with a passion for privacy. The one characteristic often remarked upon by those who worked with him was that his work ethic consisted of one almost fanatical and inhuman premise: "Stop when all work is done—and not before." This did not endear him to many of his former wardrobe men and women, as might be imagined, although it did earn him the respect of his colleagues.

Bill Theiss was born in San Francisco on November 20 of either 1930 or 1931. He graduated from Stanford University in 1953 with a bachelor's degree in art, from the Art Center College of Design. His first job in Hollywood was serving as secretary to actor Cary Grant. Theiss credits Grant's ex-wife, actress Dyan Cannon, with having a major influence on his long and varied career.

We know that during the time of *Star Trek*, Bill lived in an apartment on Westbourne Avenue, near Desilu Studios, now the Paramount Studio.

A small office was Theiss's working space. First he settled in the old RKO Wardrobe Department (the building no longer exists) across from the small "swing," or extra, *Star Trek* stage. Later, his office was in a section of a large building in the center of the studio. He would dream and sketch and then draw and clothe the inhabitants of the galaxy. Meanwhile, in the next workroom, Pat, Geneva, Pauline, Joy, and many others fashioned the costumes he had envisioned.

With worry over lack of time and money as his constant companion, Bill had patience for no one: not Roddenberry, Coon, Justman—not even Solow. Bill had even less patience for anyone who stopped in to praise, criticize, comment, say hello, or say good-bye. The process could not be interrupted. Bill was rude, at times, in a supreme effort to avoid delaying the shooting company over wardrobe problems. "Better rude than late" was his motto. Although, unhappily, it wasn't often operative. Actors, extras, and wardrobe assistants remember his frenzied pinning and sewing even as the cameras began to roll.

As his colleague of four years—two of them on *Star Trek*—Andrea Weaver puts it, "Bill Theiss was a very creative designer. His designs for *Star Trek* were original rather than distilled from other sources, or redefinitions of previous works. This is what I appreciated about Bill Theiss. I thought that he was a truly unique and rare costume creator. Others may have agreed but were more influenced by Bill's personal eccentricities and rudeness. . . ."

Andrea also recalls the sewing of actors into costumes not only because the clothes wouldn't hold together any other way, but also because often they weren't really "costumes" as such. Rather, they were scraps and ribbons and wires and squares and scarves and drapes and remnants. One of the staff members of the Smithsonian Institution remembers, in preparation for the 1992 *Star Trek* exhibit, walking through the Paramount storeroom with Bill Theiss, scouring the hangers and boxes for "costumes." She was astonished to find mostly "scraps of cloth," each group neatly hanging together on one hanger, but nothing that resembled a garment!

When put together, these scraps became the legendary Theiss collection—the visually distinct portrait of *Star Trek* that remains to this day.

119

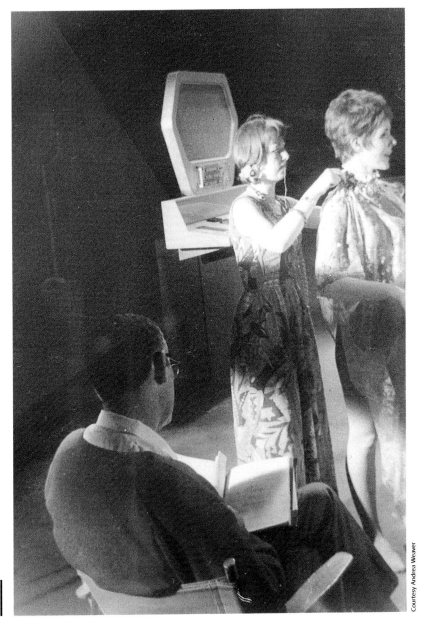

Women's costumer Andrea Weaver puts the final touches on Gem's filmy outfit on the set of "The Empath."

Courtesy Andrea Weaver

The jumpsuit—a favorite design of Bill Theiss, for males—worn by Roger Korby and Captain/android Kirk in "What Are Little Girls Made Of?" was one of many variations. Other incarnations are seen in "Metamorphosis," "Spock's Brain," "This Side of Paradise," and "Is There in Truth No Beauty?" to name but a few. Also, a version of this was seen as a "working" uniform for the crew of the *Enterprise*.

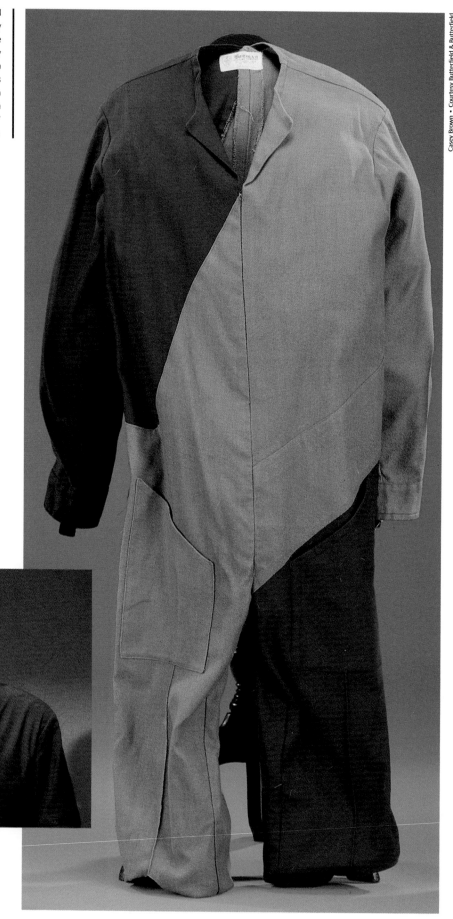

120

Paramount Pictures

Michael Strong as Roger Korby models the ubiquitous jumpsuit in "What Are Little Girls Made Of?"

These garments were worn by
madwomen, Marta in the third-season
episode "Whom Gods Destroy," and
Lethe during the first season in
"Dagger of the Mind."

One of the more improbable garments of *Star Trek*, a sleeveless fur dress worn by Lenore in "The Conscience of the King," is shown with another of her garments. Karidian's robe in the same episode, featured here, was recycled later for Garth in "Whom Gods Destroy."

The robes of the actor,
Anton Karidian (Arnold Moss),
can not hide Kodos
from his accuser.

123

The "lost Lenore," played
by Barbara Anderson.

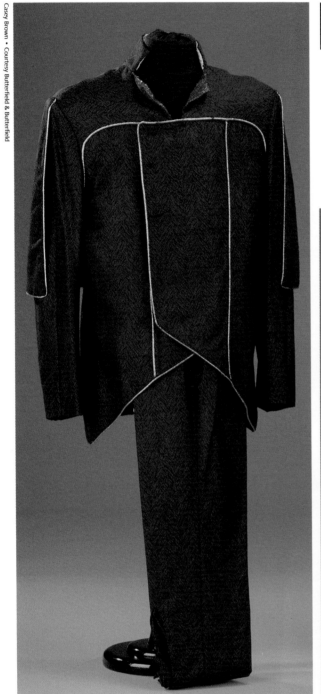

John Crawford as Commissioner Ferris, an officious passenger aboard the *Enterprise*, dons this suitable raiment in "The Galileo Seven."

124

Another fabulous jumpsuit, reconfigured by Bill Theiss in his never-ending attempt to "cut the coat to fit the cloth/budget." This one was worn by Spock and the colonists in "This Side of Paradise."

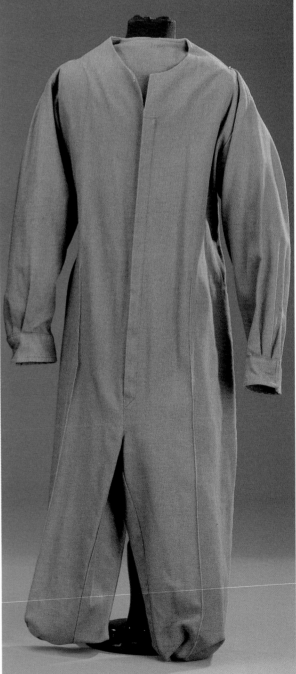

Frank Overton as Elias Sandoval
wearing a jumpsuit that echoes mindless
uniformity of the spores' control.

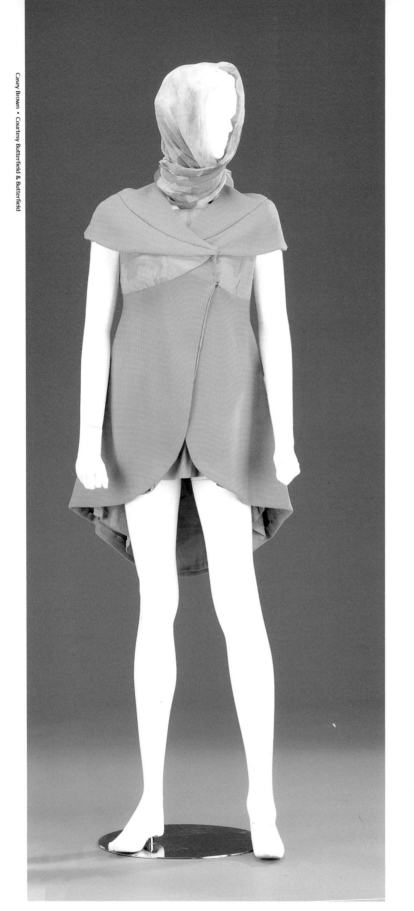

Designed for the part of Commissioner Hedford in "Metamorphosis," this "dress" was in reality a series of scraps held precariously together for the duration of shooting.

Actress Elinor Donahue as Commissioner Hedford; the translucent
scarf was used by the Commissioner/Companion to view "the man"
in the manner to which she was previously accustomed.

Perhaps one of Bill Theiss's most recognized
creations, the "Greek" gown fashioned for
"Who Mourns for Adonais?"

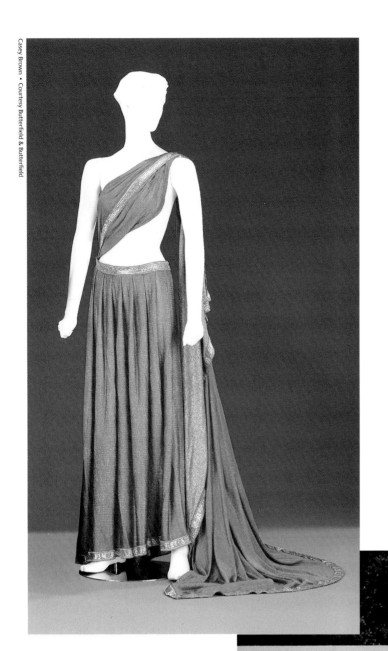

As you can see from the costume, and from the actress playing Lieutenant Palamas (Leslie Parrish), the design was daring not only in what it showed but in how it was worn by the actress.

129

Many costume sketches were or had to be drastically changed for various reasons before they were turned into actual garments. This, however, was not one of them.

The guards prepare to enforce T'Pring's (Arlene Martel) *kal-if-fee*.

Space
Hocker

Previously thought to be a sketch rejected for "Mudd's Women," this costume was worn by a waitress in the bar scene for "Wolf in the Fold."

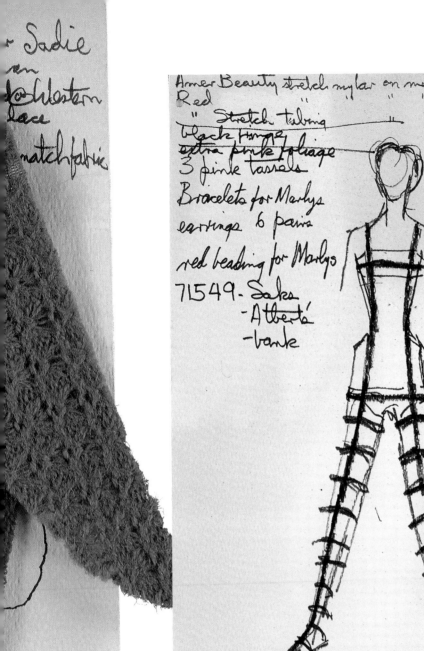

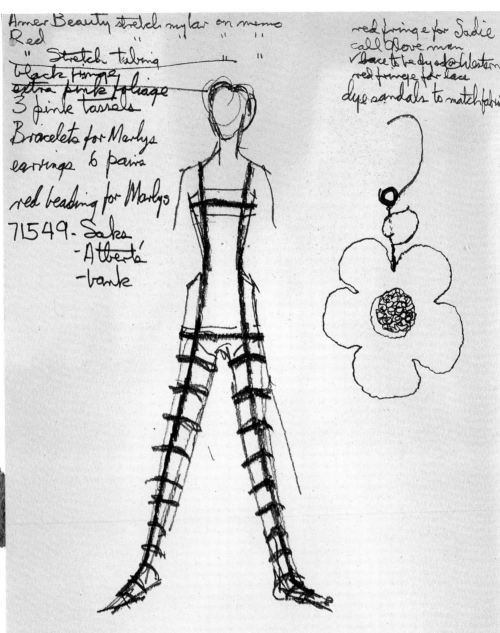

As many creative people do, Bill Theiss made notes for himself on whatever piece of paper was at hand. On this sketch, for "Elaan of Troyius," Bill's phone list includes "Sadie" (Sadie Mintz, who, with her husband Sid, rented jewelry to *Star Trek*); Albert's, which was a hosiery supplier in Hollywood; and the bank, as usual. As for Marlys, no one can recall the name.

Among these swatches are pieces of costumes *Star Trek* fans will recognize from "The Deadly Years," "Bread and Circuses," and "The Way to Eden." Attaching fabric to a sketch is done to provide suggested material and colors for the people cutting and sewing the costumes.

133

This is a sketch for the mystic Sybo's seance dress, in "Wolf in the Fold."

135

These unappealing draperies were made for Dr. Janet Wallace in "The Deadly Years." They resurfaced during the third season in "And the Children Shall Lead."

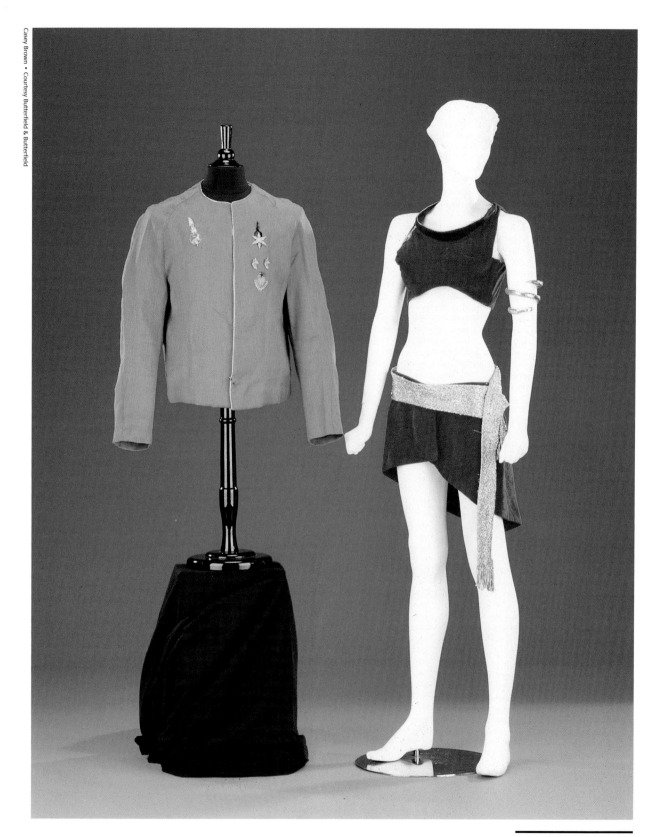

The alternate universe
uniforms for Spock and Uhura,
designed for "Mirror, Mirror."

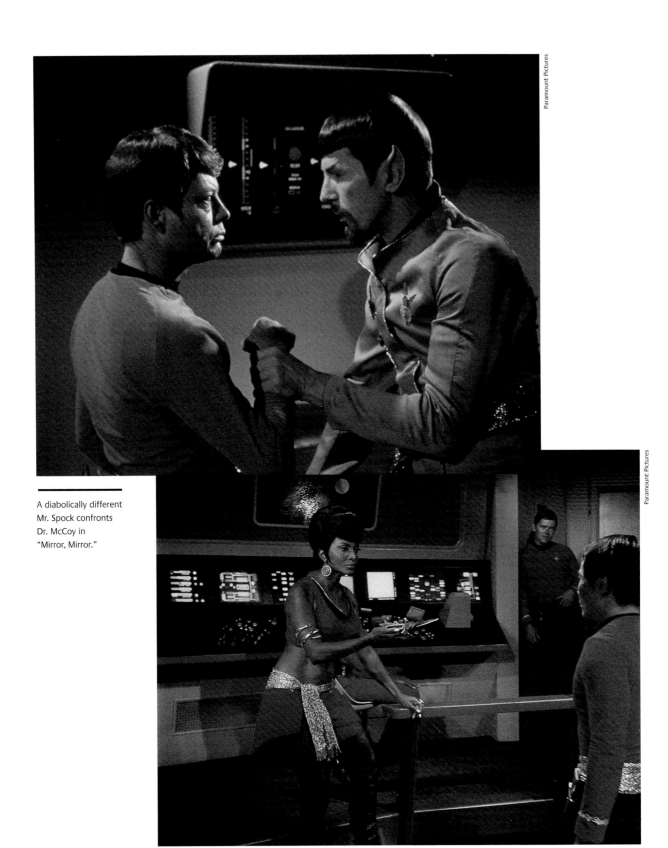

A diabolically different
Mr. Spock confronts
Dr. McCoy in
"Mirror, Mirror."

137

Uhura fends off an
unwanted suitor.

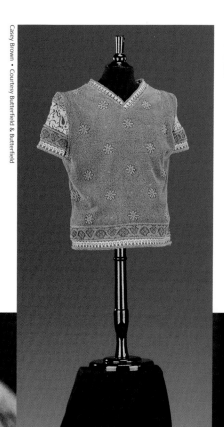

Captain Merrick, former commander of the *S.S. Beagle*, is transformed by his own weakness, and by Bill Theiss's excellent costuming, into First Citizen Merickus.

R.M. Merrick (William Smithers) swagger is evident as the clothes make him into First Citizen Merikus.

This unlikely garment, a prototype for Flavius's in "Bread and Circuses," never quite made it. An outfit reminiscent of this sketch appears on another gladiator.

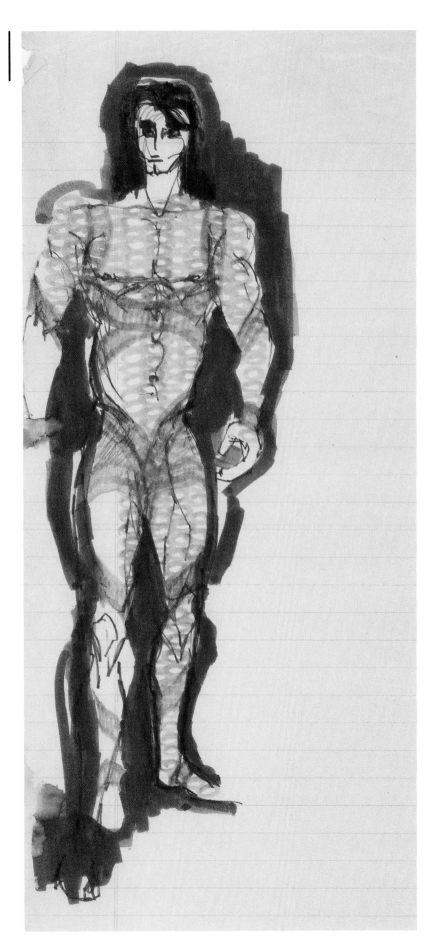

Mark Lenard as Sarek and Jane
Wyatt as Amanda, whose
grace, poise and intelligence
personify Spock's parents.

Sarek and Amanda augment their
Vulcan demeanor and dignity with a
little fire in this highly crafted clothing
from the episode "Journey to Babel."

ch 1A
Trinito

A chic outfit for Spock's mother, equally suitable for lunching in the city or traveling through space with murderous aliens. Note the detail on the back.

This interesting collar was unfortunately not used in the final design. A faint note written by Bill Theiss appears in the bottom right-hand corner.

Wearing a subdued version of Theiss's original design, Amanda seeks out her son aboard the *Enterprise*.

Casey Brown • Courtesy Butterfield & Butterfield

Paramount Pictures

This dress was important, since it was
worn by a character, Roberta Lincoln,
who was intended to be the co-star of
a new television series. The episode,
"Assignment: Earth," was a "backdoor"
pilot. It doubled as a *Star Trek* episode
and the prototype for a potential series.

The mid-sixties are reflected visually whenever
Roberta appears. The colors and material Theiss
used for this dress, although mildly "psychedelic,"
are really quite mainstream for the time.

Elaan, it seems, was fond of clothes, since she had more costume changes than any other guest star. This sketch was rendered almost exactly as planned.

France Nuyen as Elaan the Dohlman of Elas. The unparalleled style of Bill's costume is enhanced by the actress.

Theiss imagined quite a different costume
for the Ambassador from Troyius. It seems
that he was, as his employers put it,
"designing without budget in mind."

The Dohlman's guard's costume ended
up even more dramatic than this sketch,
although less expensive.

STAR TREK

HELEN OF TROYIUS

by

J... Meredyth Lucas

STORY OUTLINE
March 22, 1968

This sketch for the front of Elaan's costume was done on the cover of the story outline for "Elaan of Troyius," likely a case of using paper available when the idea occurred.

The back of the same costume.

The actual outfit for Ambassador Petri
and one of Theiss's typically revealing
creations for the Dohlman Elaan.

Miramanee might have looked stunning in this Theiss design. The final costume was created along the lines of more traditional Hollywood prototypes.

Miramanee

153

The Romulan commander's uniform from "The Enterprise Incident." It was patterned after the male Romulan costume, but like those of her Federation counterparts, it revealed more of her form.

The manifestation of the above sketch, shown here with the Romulan commander's "something more comfortable," demonstrates one of the few instances when Theiss's sketch and the resultant costume were identical.

The children of Triacus, who scamper unconcernedly among the dead bodies of their parents, in their Theiss-designed playsuits, from "And the Children Shall Lead."

This jumpsuit exhibits
a streamlined effect, next
to the marvelous sensor
gown created for the blind
Doctor Miranda Jones.

Scribbles of jumpsuits sprout prolifically
among Bill Theiss's drawings. This sketch—
done for Larry Mavrick for "Is There in Truth
No Beauty?"—is a variation of the same
garment seen throughout the series.

Casey Brown • Courtesy Butterfield & Butterfield

Natira's attire, in "For the World Is Hollow and I Have Touched the Sky," was another of those arrangement of scraps that managed to work so well on *Star Trek*. This sketch, like many others, was indeed done on a napkin.

Although these male costumes from "Wink of an Eye" appear diminutive in this photo, it is only because the pants, three quarters in length, tucked into the boots. Bill Theiss had an aversion to metallic fabrics, but he often said that there wasn't much alternative in the sixties for "alien material."

Kathie Browne as Deela. This photo shows her dramatic costume and the "actor's marks."

From left to right, wardrobe from "The Mark of Gideon" for a council member, Krodak, Odona, and Hodin. Odona's clothing is a composite of a number of sketches.

Casey Brown • Courtesy Butterfield & Butterfield

163

As with many of Theiss's designs, the finished garment for Droxine in "The Cloud Minders" surpassed his sketches, and was more flattering on the actress than on the mannequin shown here. The male costume appears equally flattering.

Casey Brown • Courtesy Butterfield & Butterfield

Irina's costume underwent dramatic change in its evolution—from stripes to flowers, from fairly rigid to flowing fabric—in this "flower child" episode, "The Way to Eden."

Irina's final costume, along with those of her companions, Mavig and Tongo Rad. The choice of fabric and color was heavily influenced by the contemporary designs of the late sixties.

Surak, the father of Vulcan philosophy, wears his pedagogical robes with ironic grace. The final garment seen in "Savage Curtain" seems subdued by comparison.

Surak

BILL RETURNED TO STAR TREK

TO DESIGN THE

INITIAL CREW UNIFORMS

AND COSTUMES FOR THE

FIRST YEAR OF STAR TREK:

THE NEXT GENERATION.

THOSE WHO KNEW

BILL PERSONALLY IN

HIS LATER YEARS

REMEMBER HIM AS

AN INTELLIGENT, WITTY,

AND ENTERTAINING

CONVERSATIONALIST—

STILL IMPATIENT, STILL

CONTENTIOUS—AND

STILL VERY PRIVATE.

FRED PHILLIPS

It was Monday morning on a summer day in 1966 at Desilu Studios in Hollywood. Fred Phillips, makeup artist for the new *Star Trek* series, sat in his one-room makeup department, sipping coffee. As was his usual procedure, he began his day by looking over several new story outlines for future episodes, which had been placed in his mail tray sometime over the weekend.

Fred smiled and murmured to himself, "Solow, Coon, Roddenberry, and Justman are working overtime again." Suddenly, Fred lowered his coffee cup and reread a few lines from two of the outlines. He quickly grabbed a pad of paper and a pencil and wrote down several words: "Klingon—Romulan—alien races—conceptualize them—design them—make them." And knowing the *Star Trek* production world, Fred added the word "fast."

168

But for the man who in 1927, with a flour and water paste, applied eyelashes one by one to the stars of Cecil B. DeMille's film *King of Kings*; for the man who in 1931 made up Frederic March for the original *Dr. Jekyll and Mr. Hyde*; for the man who in 1967 turned actors into primates for *The Planet of the Apes*; and for the man who made up the stars of over one hundred films, it was just another day at the office.

FREDERICK

BEAUREGARD

PHILLIPS

WAS THE

RIGHT MAN

FOR THE

RIGHT JOB

AT THE

RIGHT TIME.

Fred Phillips was born in Raleigh, North Carolina, in 1908 and moved to Hollywood at age three when his father, Festus Beauregard Phillips, became a silent picture actor. It was a time when actors applied their own makeup, and Festus became expert at applying everything. But when Festus Phillips's Southern accent failed to translate to "talkies," he became a full-time makeup artist. Along with fellow makeup artist Perc Westmore, Festus Phillips founded the Motion Picture Makeup Artists' Association.

Fred Phillips loved going to the studio with his father. At age fourteen, Fred became a makeup apprentice. When actor Russell Simpson's car broke down, Freddie gave him a ride to the old Hampton Studios. Simpson was taken with the young man's resourcefulness and convinced the studio to hire him. Ten years later, Fred Phillips was the entire makeup department on *Face in the Sky*; part of his job was making up horses.

Fred Phillips makes up Nelson Eddy in the star's dressing room for a role in *Naughty Marietta* (1934). This was one of several films on which Freddie worked with Nelson Eddy.

Fred Phillips works on Ray Milland on the location set of *Bugles in the Afternoon* (1952).

Fred Phillips and Boris Karloff on the set of *The Man with Nine Lives* (1940).

MANY OF THE LEADING FEMALE STARS OF THE 1930'S AND 40'S REQUESTED FRED PHILLIPS AS THEIR MAKEUP ARTIST.

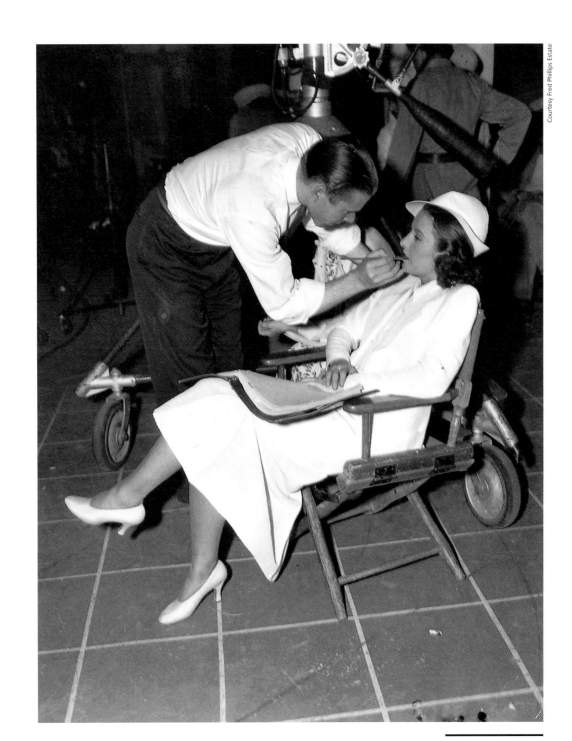

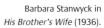

173

Barbara Stanwyck in
His Brother's Wife (1936).

Jeanette MacDonald in
Rose Marie (1935).

Loretta Young from
Men in Her Life (1941).

OTHER LEADING LADIES MADE UP BY FREDDIE INCLUDED
CLARA BOW, JEAN HARLOW, LUISE RAINER, JEAN ARTHUR,
NORMA SHEARER, CAROLE LOMBARD, MARLENE DIETRICH,
RITA HAYWORTH, PAULETTE GODDARD, TEXAS GUINAN,
JANET GAYNOR, GRETA GARBO, SHIRLEY TEMPLE, ALICE FAY,
SUSAN HAYWARD, AND JOAN BLONDELL.

Rosalind Russell in
*Mourning Becomes
Electra* (1946). Freddie
is "giving" Rosalind
Russell a jawline with
his use of shading.

Dame Judith Anderson appeared in *The Outer Limits* in 1963. This was Fred's first venture into television science fiction.

AFTER TWO YEARS OF WORK ON THE VERY SUCCESSFUL ABC SERIES THE OUTER LIMITS, FREDDIE PHILLIPS WAS WELL PREPARED FOR STAR TREK'S *FIRST PILOT, "THE CAGE."*

177

The initial *Star Trek* makeup and appliance task given to Fred Phillips was to create the inhabitants of Talos IV for "The Cage." His Talosians, with their pulsating brains and minute ears, were an instant hit.

The first of many Neanderthal types the *Enterprise* crew would run into across the galaxy. Kaylar from "The Cage" has a distinctly Viking flair.

Courtesy Greg Jein

Someone's idea of "sexy" necessitated gobs of greasy green skin makeup: an endless process, since every time the actress perspired, the makeup would blotch, cake, and run off.

Vina's surface beauty begins to diminish when the Talosians allow reality to intrude, in the first moments of this poignant scene from "The Cage."

179

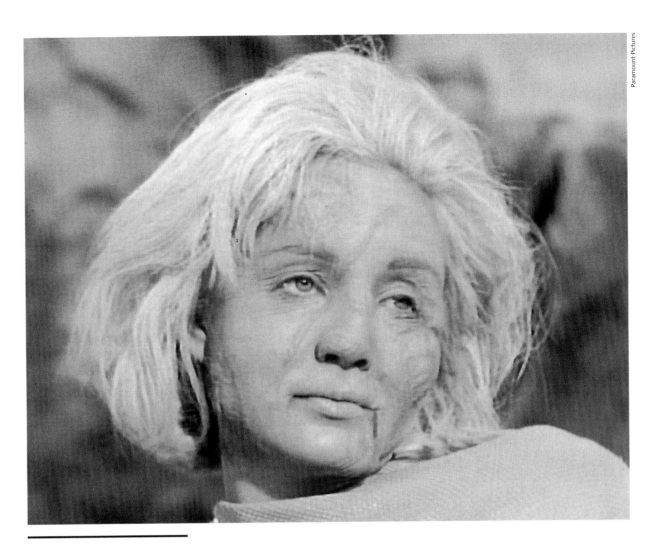

Paramount Pictures

Vina's misshapen body in this transforma-
tion scene owes its form to the Talosians'
lack of familiarity with humans, and to
Fred Phillips's imaginative approach.

The youthful vigor drains from Vina's face, as
she begins to see herself as she appears to
Captain Pike. Note the very subtle changes
Freddie made in order to achieve this effect.

FREDDIE WAS CHALLENGED TO MAKE UP "THE GALAXY," IN STAR TREK: THE ORIGINAL SERIES.

Turning Leonard Nimoy into Mr. Spock took approximately ninety minutes. In a crunch, Freddie would put everything else aside and concentrate solely on Spock. His record time was forty-nine minutes.
Courtesy of Stephen Edward Poe

Freddie's skill with Spock's ears and eyebrows stood him in good stead with the entire Romulan crew. Here, actors Mark Lenard and John Warburton as the Romulan Commander and the Centurion. The Romulans are presented as an ancient scion of the Vulcan race, in "Balance of Terror."

185

A formidable adversary, Ruk the android from
"What Are Little Girls Made Of?" shows off
Freddie's diverse makeup skills. The ghastly pale
makeup reinforces Ruk's otherworldliness.

Paramount Pictures

Creation of a deadly disease that scars and then kills adults, in "Miri," was a simple matter for Freddie. It was his choice of color that added the dramatic edge.

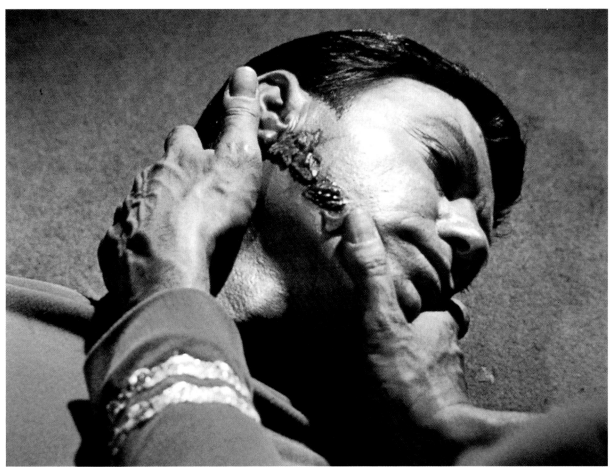

Paramount Pictures

187

The first pilot star, Jeffrey Hunter, was unwilling to do further shooting for the remake of "The Cage" into a two-part episode, "The Menagerie." A dramatic device was employed to disfigure Captain Pike beyond recognition, so that a different actor could be used as Hunter's replacement. Sean Kenney was the "after the accident" actor. Note Sean's inscription to Freddie: "To Fred—Thank you for your wonderful 'Face Lift'—Love & Happiness—Sean Kenney."

188

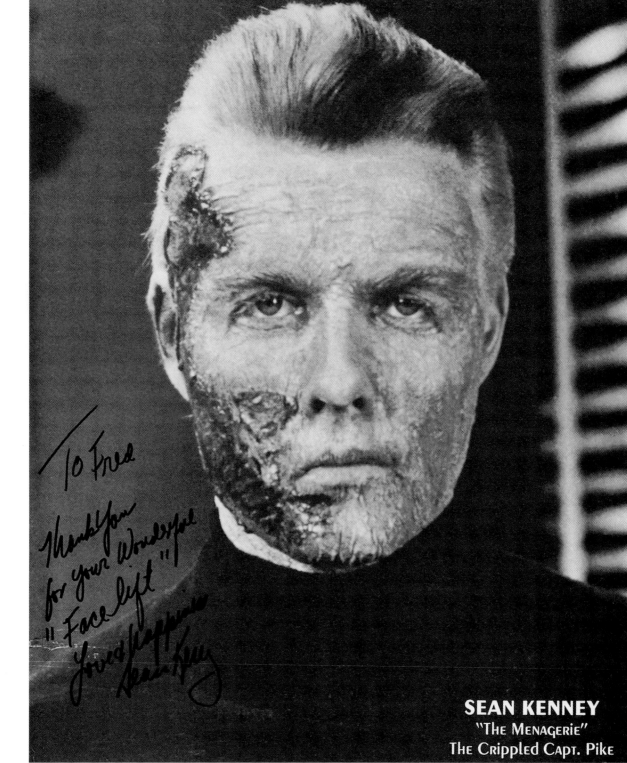

SEAN KENNEY
"THE MENAGERIE"
The Crippled Capt. Pike

William Shatner and DeForest Kelley have aged far more gracefully in real life than in this publicity photo from "The Deadly Years."

189

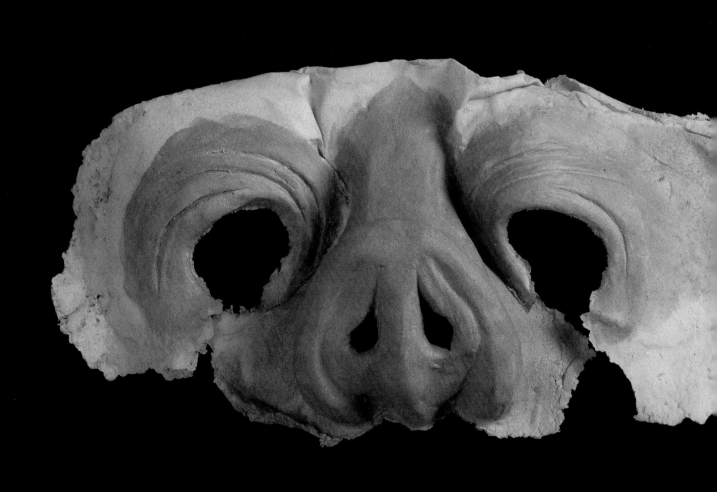

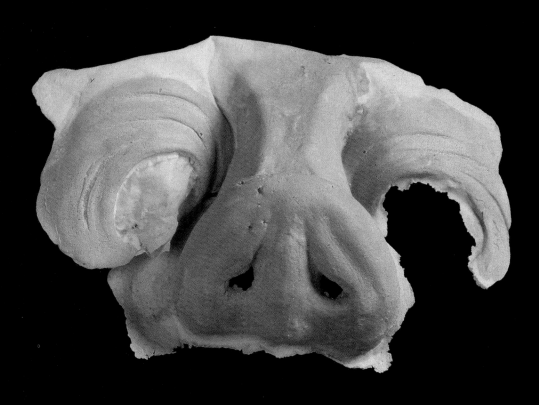

Freddie's expertise in the area of an actor's physiognomy wasn't utilized only on ears. Here are two nose appliances that Freddie created and manufactured for the Tellarites in "Journey to Babel." Note that they have not yet been colored to coincide with the final skin tone of the character. Courtesy Fred Phillips Estate

192

The Tellarite, Gav, comes to
life courtesy of Phillips's skill.

Note Freddie's Talosian-like Vian makeup in "The Empath." Robert Justman and other personnel appear in the foreground.

193

Dr. Sevrin from "The Way to Eden" gives new meaning to the phrase "cauliflower ears." This is an example of the cuts made in the third season makeup budget.

194

ONCE A MAKEUP ARTIST DECIDES, WITH THE ABLE ASSISTANCE OF THE PRODUCER, THE DIRECTOR, AND THE CAMERAMAN, HOW HIS SUBJECT SHOULD LOOK, THAT "LOOK" MUST BE RE-CREATED EACH AND EVERY DAY. MAKEUP ARTISTS WERE GIVEN FILM STRIPS TO HOLD UP TO LIGHT AND "SQUINT AT" IN ORDER TO DETERMINE UNIFORMITY.

Gene Coon created the Klingons and their culture, but Fred Phillips created the look of the Klingons. Here, in a film strip makeup check, is actor John Colicos from the episode "Errand of Mercy."

Courtesy Fred Phillips Estate

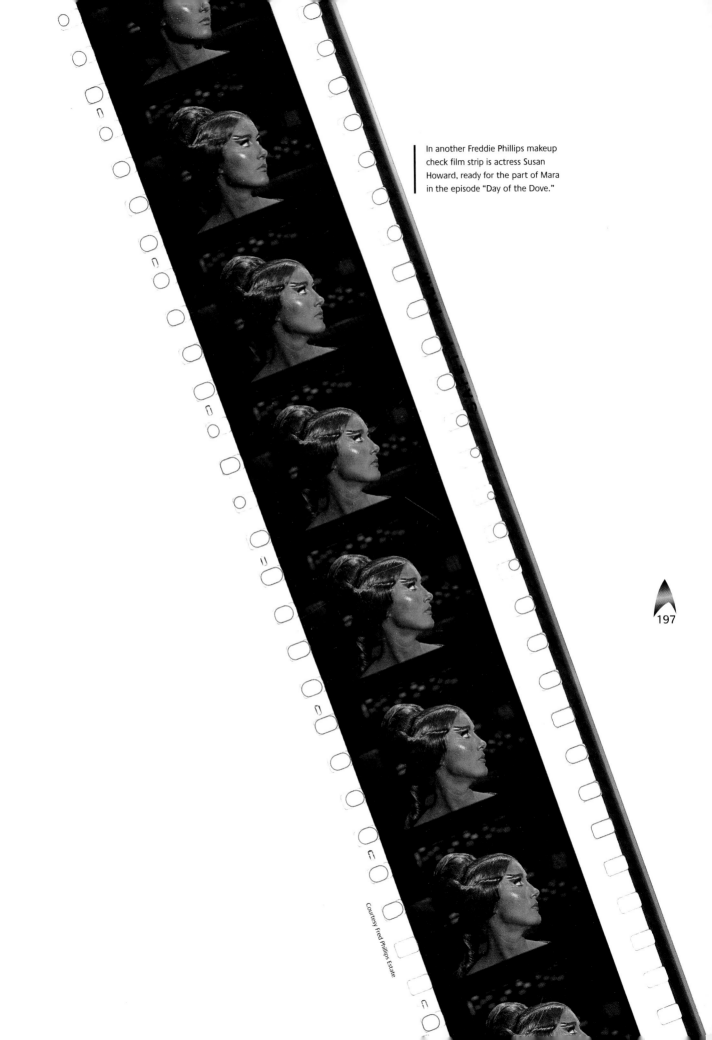

In another Freddie Phillips makeup check film strip is actress Susan Howard, ready for the part of Mara in the episode "Day of the Dove."

Courtesy Fred Phillips Estate

LIFE FOR FREDDIE PHILLIPS AFTER THE STAR TREK SERIES MEANT GOING BACK TO THE FREELANCE WORLD. THERE WERE SOME OTHER CHANGES, THOUGH NOT IN MAKEUP OR JOBS. THE ADVENT OF THE POLAROID CAMERA PROVED TO BE A BLESSING TO MAKEUP ARTISTS. A QUICK "MAKEUP CHECK PHOTO" WAS A VALUABLE VISUAL TOOL FROM WHICH TO WORK. FREDDIE PHILLIPS MADE GOOD USE OF HIS POLAROID CAMERA.

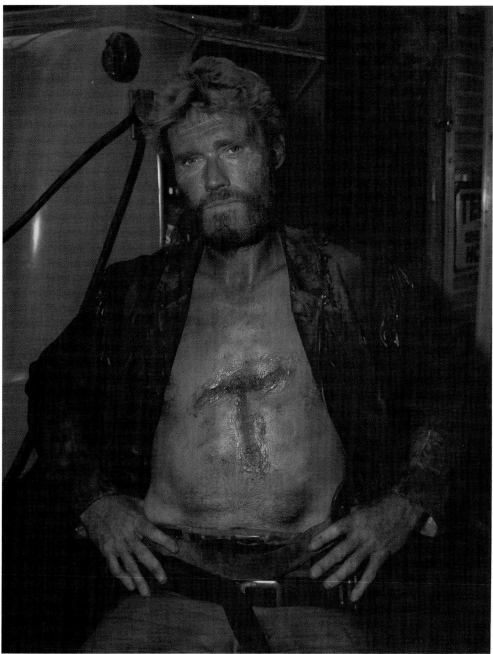

Chuck Connors takes a beating in *Ride Beyond Vengeance*, a 1965 western.

Courtesy Fred Phillips Estate

Makeup check photo of Burl Ives,
an actor-balladeer from the 1968
movie *McMasters*.

Mark Harris, the last inhabitant of Atlantis, played by actor Patrick Duffy, could live underwater, thanks in part to his webbed hands. Courtesy Fred Phillips Estate

Freddie hadn't yet finished with *Star Trek*. He
would leave the freelance world behind and
return to the *Star Trek* world, to be in charge of
the makeup on *Star Trek: The Motion Picture* (1978).

204

Welcome back, Fred!
Happy Holidays 1978

Gene Roddenberry

Courtesy Fred Phillips Estate

It started with a "welcome back"
from Gene Roddenberry.

Many times, Freddie Phillips, makeup artist, was
also a sculptor. After the plaster mold was com-
pleted, Freddie would cast a latex mask from it.

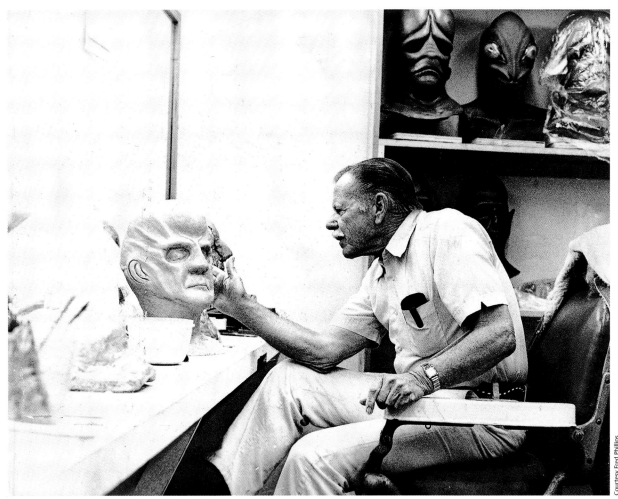

205

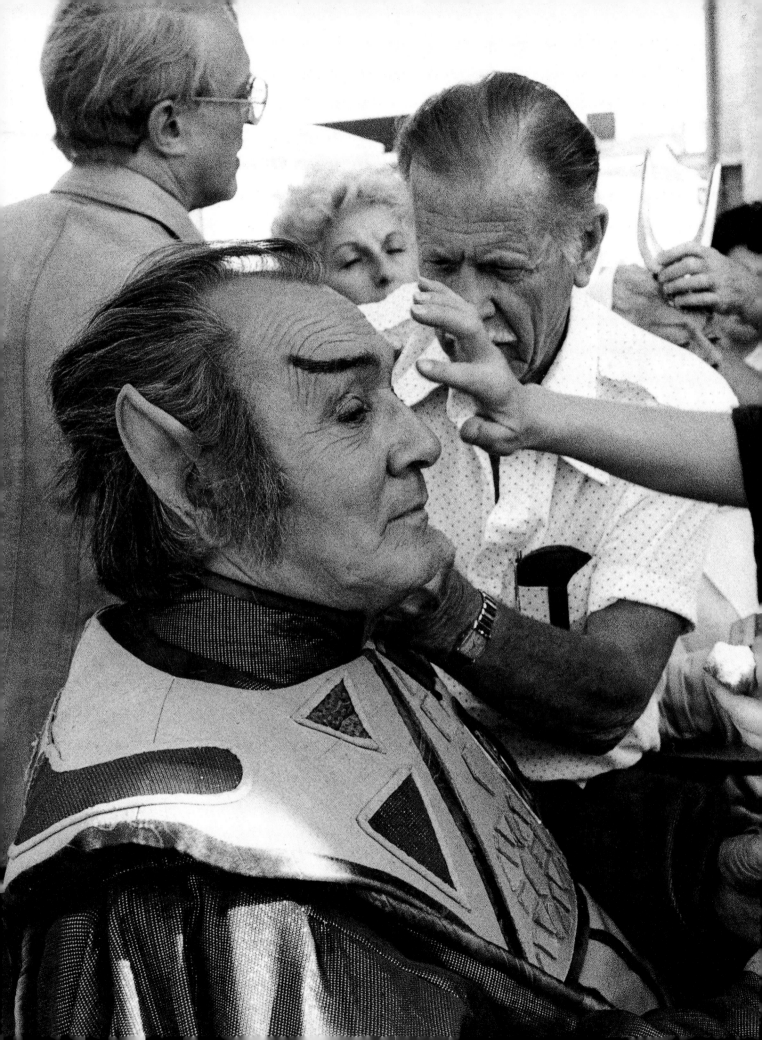

Freddie and one of his
assistant makeup artists
touch up a Vulcan master.

207

Courtesy Fred Phillips Estate

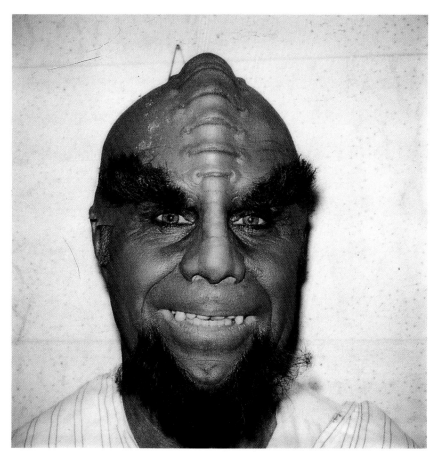

Courtesy Fred Phillips Estate

Courtesy Fred Phillips Estate

The need for a big-screen version of the Klingons created an opportunity for Freddie, with more time and money to add "character" to his alien creations. Note the addition of dental appliances to the Klingons.

The first appearance of
the Klingons in movies.

The lovely Lt. Uhura, Nichelle
Nichols, in the makeup room,
with an interesting choice of
wall decoration.

Actress Persis Khambatta, just prior to receiving her new look.

Persis waits patiently for the plaster to dry, as a mold of her head is created.

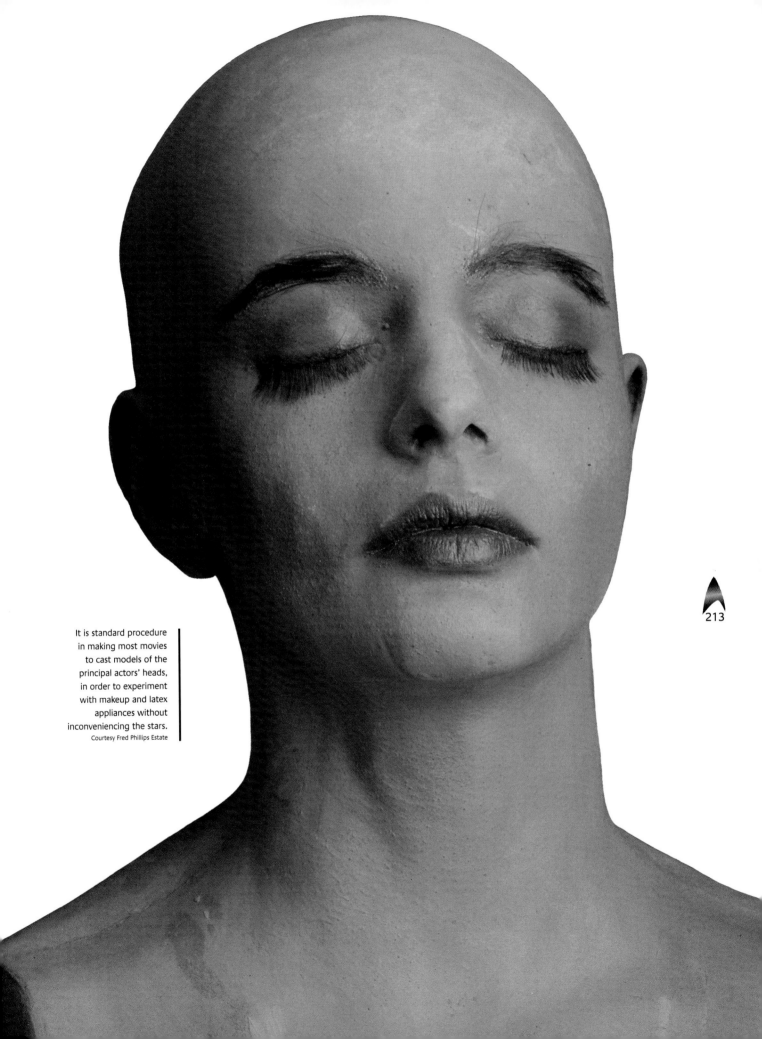

It is standard procedure
in making most movies
to cast models of the
principal actors' heads,
in order to experiment
with makeup and latex
appliances without
inconveniencing the stars.
Courtesy Fred Phillips Estate

213

The model of Persis Khambatta
was also useful for trying out
different wardrobe styles.

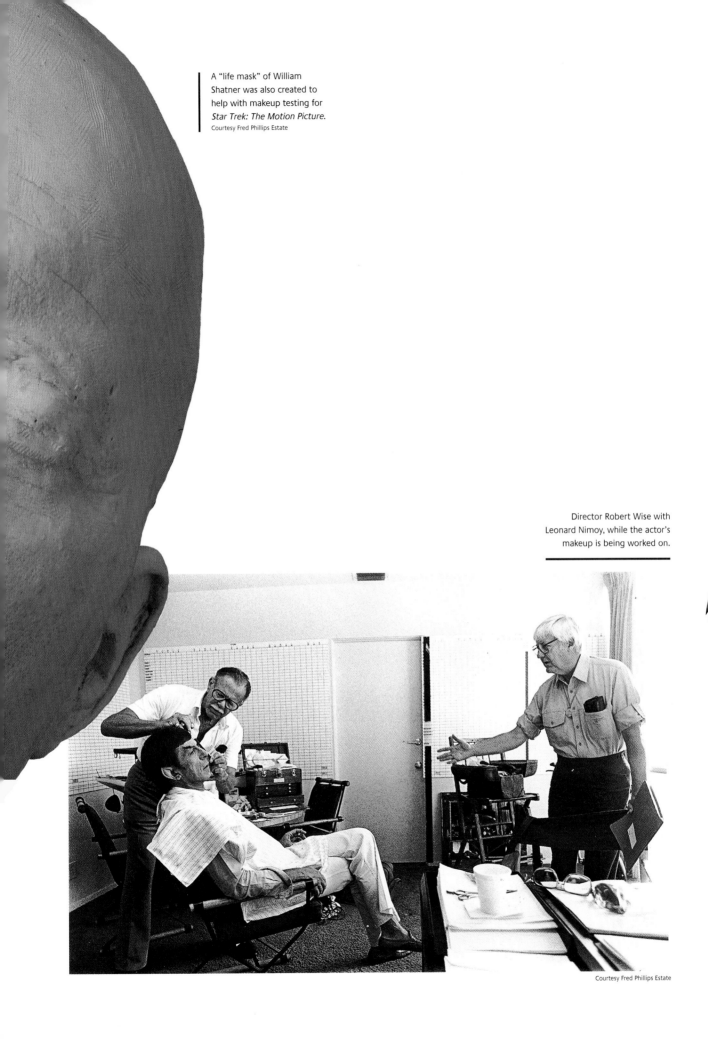

A "life mask" of William Shatner was also created to help with makeup testing for *Star Trek: The Motion Picture.*
Courtesy Fred Phillips Estate

Director Robert Wise with Leonard Nimoy, while the actor's makeup is being worked on.

215

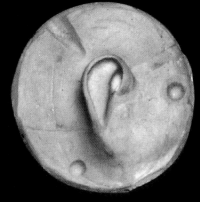

Two examples of the three-part mold process that began the process intended to result in usable Spock ears. The critical factor was the seam between the bottom of the Spock ear and the top of Leonard Nimoy's ear.

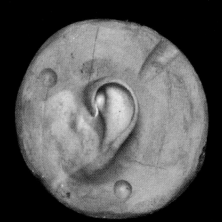

216

Not all of Freddie's attempts at Mr. Spock's ears were successful. Here are two Spock ear appliances that failed to make the grade due to look, size, comfort, or fit.

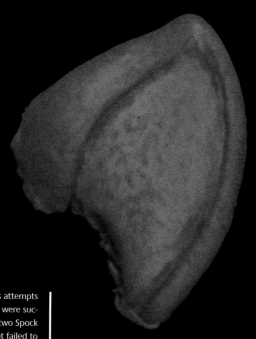
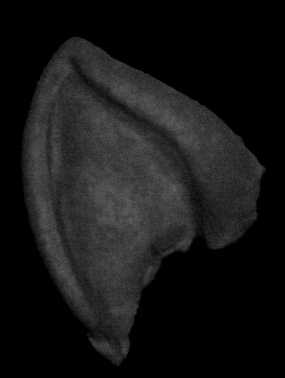

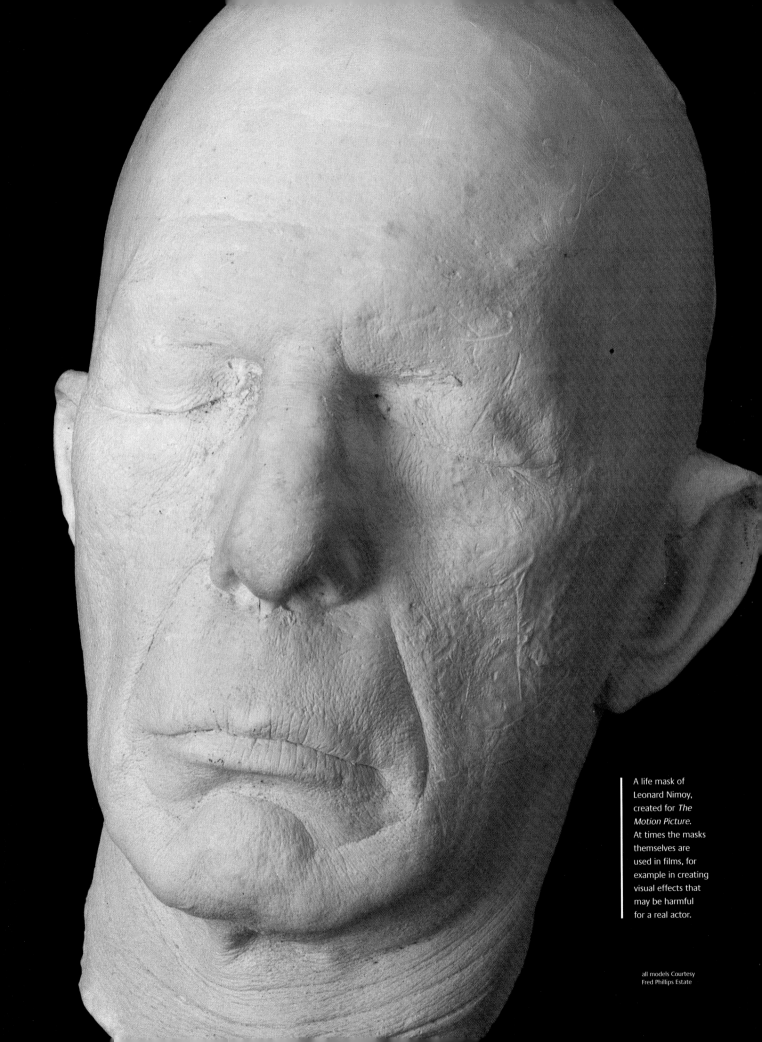

A life mask of
Leonard Nimoy,
created for *The
Motion Picture*.
At times the masks
themselves are
used in films, for
example in creating
visual effects that
may be harmful
for a real actor.

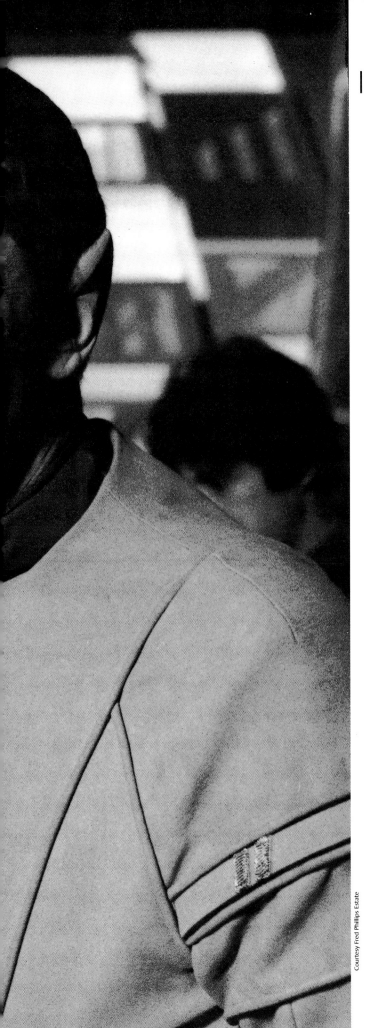

Freddie with the *Star Trek* icon he helped create, Mr. Spock.

219

FREDDIE WAS ASKED TO REPEAT HIS MAKEUP ROLE FOR STAR TREK II: THE WRATH OF KHAN. DUE TO HIS FAILING EYESIGHT AND HIS PROBLEMS WITH DEPTH PERCEPTION, FREDDIE WAS FORCED TO TURN DOWN THE OFFER. IT WAS THE MAJOR DISAPPOINTMENT OF HIS LIFE. SHORTLY THEREAFTER, FRED PHILLIPS RETIRED FROM ACTIVE PARTICIPATION IN THE FILM AND TELEVISION INDUSTRIES.

ON AUGUST 20, 1983, FRED RECEIVED THE LIFETIME ACHIEVEMENT AWARD FOR MAKEUP FROM THE SOCIETY OF OPERATING CAMERAMEN.

Phillips died on March 21, 1993. Jean Phillips, Freddie's wife of 27 years, died on September 6, 1996.

WAH MING CHANG

Wah Ming Chang was born in Honolulu in 1917 to Dai Song and Fai Sue Chang. Seven years later, the family moved from Honolulu to San Francisco, where Wah's parents would manage the Ho Ho Tea Room, at 315 Sutter Street, a popular sanctuary for many of San Francisco's avant-garde artists and writers.

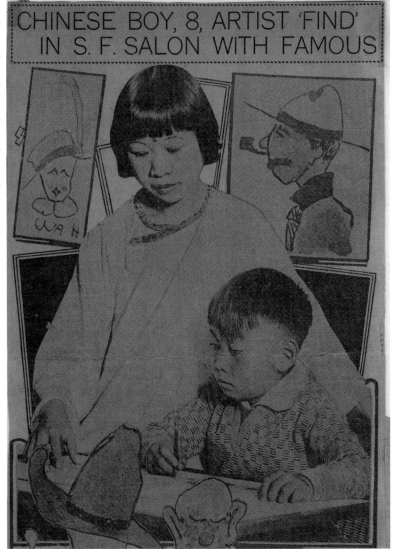

CHINESE BOY, 8, ARTIST 'FIND'
IN S. F. SALON WITH FAMOUS

With his mother who was a graduate of the California School of Arts and Crafts, in Oakland, California, and a father who studied architecture and etching, a very young Wah Chang soon became an integral part of the local art scene.

Courtesy Wah Chang

At the tender age of six, Wah's talents and abilities at painting, etching, and sculpting exploded onto the West Coast art world. A year later, Wah Chang was exhibiting regularly at San Francisco galleries.

The New York Times

AN INFANT PRODIGY FROM CHINA: WAH MING CHANG, 8, Who Recently Gave a "One Man Show" of His Artistic Creations at a Gallery in San Francisco, Where His Ability Received High Commendation From Critics.

(Times Wide World Photos, San Fracinsco Bureau.)

By the time he was ten years old, Wah Chang's fame had spread to the East Coast. One of his prints was accepted by the Brooklyn Society of Etchers and was exhibited alongside the work of Frank Duveneck and James McNeill Whistler. That same year, Wah's work was exhibited at the Annual Show of the Philadelphia Print Club.

June 1936

SAN FR

Chinese Youngster at Age Of Eight Puts Name High In Ranks of Child Artists

Wah Ming Chang Draws Illustrations for His Own Stories

Every boy likes cowboys and Indians, but there aren't many who can illustrate their own Wild West stories.

That's where Wah Ming Chang, 8-year-old son of Mrs. Sue Chang, has it on the rest of boytown. When he was 2 years old he scrawled stiff little sketches of lambs to slip un-

Wah Ming Chang, aged 8, already has to his credit a "one man show" of pictures which show him to have ability far beyond the average.

224

Courtesy Wah Chang

At sixteen, Wah Chang was put in charge of building several sets at the famous Hollywood Bowl. He also contributed to a puppet movie produced and directed by Leroy Prinz.

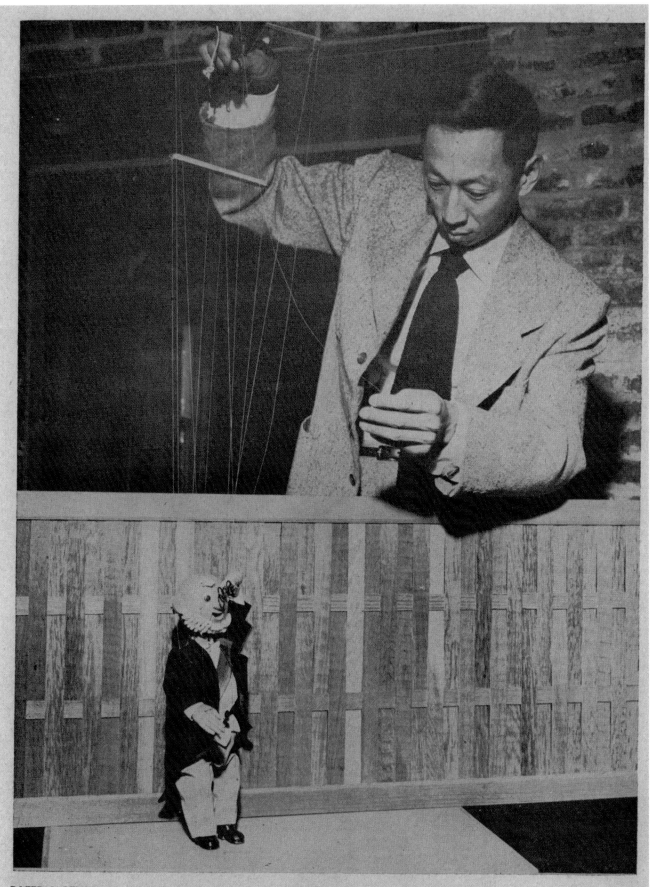

225

RATED A GENIUS from the time he was 9, Wah Chang was creating puppets professionally while he was still in school.

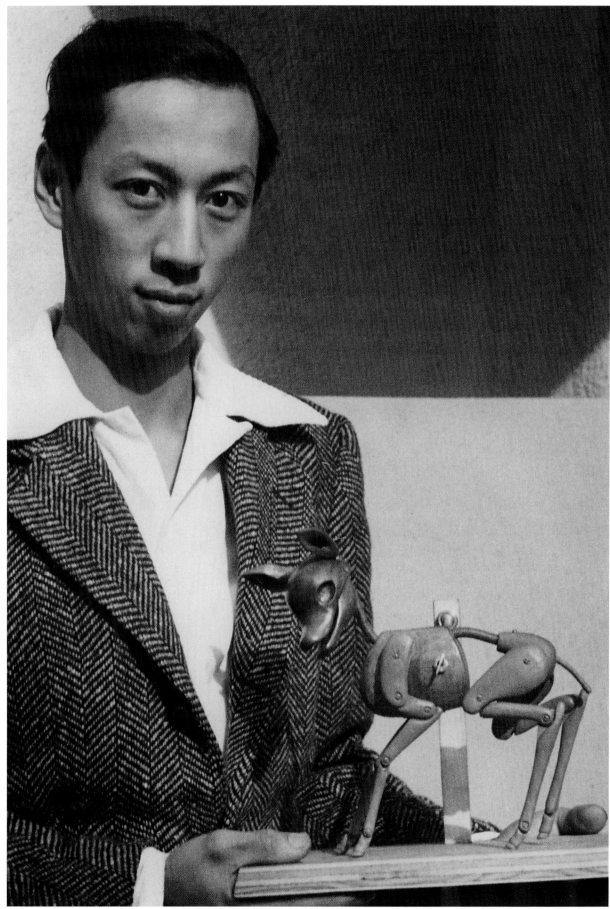

226

Four years later Wah was "found" by Hollywood. He was hired by Disney Studios' Effects and Model Departments. He was then assigned to the design and construction of special effects and puppets for *Pinocchio*, *Fantasia*, and *Bambi*. This is Wah's action puppet used to assist Disney animators in visualizing Bambi's movements.

Tragedy befell Wah Chang. Stricken with polio, he had to spend many painful months in a local sanitarium. Within the year, Wah, fitted with metal leg braces and with the aid of a cane, was back on his feet and continuing his brilliant career.

WALT DISNEY

July 20, 1940.

Dear Wah:

It was only a few days ago that I learned of your serious illness, but I am happy to know, through Mr. Keener, that you have passed through the crisis successfully, and that you are now on the road to recovery.

It's a tough seige, I know, but I am sure you have what it takes to put you back on your feet again. We're all pulling for you here and hoping that you'll be back with us soon.

With my kindest regards and every good wish,

Sincerely,

Walt Disney

Mr. Wah Ming Chang,
Twin Oaks Sanitarium,
1302 So. Charlotte Ave.,
San Gabriel, Calif.

WD:DV

228

Wah Chang shared the Academy Award recognizing the time machine created for George Pal's film *The Time Machine*.

Congratulations

GENE WARREN

TIM BAAR

WAH CHANG

for making
"The Time Machine"
tick

H. G. Wells and his Pal, George

1960

Thirty-Third Annual Awards of Merit *by the*
ACADEMY OF MOTION PICTURE ARTS AND SCIENCES

Wah designed and manufactured
H. G. Wells's vision of a time machine.

George Pal asked Wah back to work for him on *The Wonderful World of the Brothers Grimm*. This is just one of the puppets created for the film.

Courtesy Wah Chang

Companies outside the film industry recognized Wah's special talents. Here is a case of Pillsbury "doughboy" heads. The various animated expressions were crafted by Wah.

Courtesy Wah Chang

Courtesy Wah Chang

Wah designed and manufactured masks
for the "Small House of Uncle Thomas"
sequence in the film *The King and I.*

235

Courtesy Wah Chang

Television became the predominant visual
medium in Hollywood, and Wah turned his
talents to *The Outer Limits*. It was his two
years designing and manufacturing props,
figures, and effects for this show that made
Wah feel at home in science fiction.

Desilu
PRODUCTIONS INC.

WAH MING CHANG
365 W POPPYFIELDS DR
ALTADENA CALIF

INVOICE DATE			INVOICE NUMBER	TERMS	DATE PAID			GROSS AMOUNT	DISCOUNT	VENDOR NUMBER	
MO.	DAY	YR.			MO.	DAY	YR.				
08	22	66	7761		9	25	66	520 00		0407	

Reworking Phasers

	GROSS TOTAL	DISC. TOTAL
	520 00	

CUSTOMER COPY

- 13 - P 7M 10-65 Ⓟ ˅

238

43977

ER ST.
CALIFORNIA
1

AMOUNT

520 00

In 1964, Wah came to *Star Trek* with his extraordinary talent and unparalleled credentials. Due to union complications and restrictions, however, his uncredited contributions to the 79 episodes were relatively unknown. They would have remained unknown were it not for the astonishing success of the series, and the fans' desire to know who was behind the creations of *Star Trek*.

Wah was working as a partner in the special effects and design firm Projects Unlimited during the production of the first *Star Trek* pilot, "The Cage." Thereafter, Wah dissolved his relationship with Projects Unlimited and worked independently from his home studio in Altadena, California. He soon became the "phantom" supplier of most of *Star Trek*'s alien beings and hand props.

In many instances during the production of *Star Trek*, Wah consulted with Bill Theiss when alien costume issues arose, and with Fred Phillips when special input was required on particular alien makeup. This synergetic relationship accounted for fewer hands making better products in less time, a key *Star Trek* design necessity.

Courtesy Wah Chang

NET TOTAL

520 00

Wah charged Desilu a very modest $1,019.20 for designing and making two practical and eight dummy communicators.

The phasers designed by Matt and John Jefferies were manufactured by Wah for $520.00.

Desilu
PRODUCTIONS INC.

780 N
HOLL
HOLLY
CHECK #

WAH MING CHANG
365 W POPPYFIELDS DR
ALTADENA CALIF

INVOICE DATE			INVOICE NUMBER	TERMS	DATE PAID			GROSS AMOUNT	DISCOUNT	VENDOR NUMBER	
MO.	DAY	YR.			MO.	DAY	YR.				
07	26	66	8620		8	10	66	748 80		0845	

Pd 8/13/66
Helmets &
Ears -

Helmet & ears

240

		GROSS TOTAL	DISC. TOTAL	
CUSTOMER COPY		748 80		9

13 - P 7M 10-65 ℗ ∨

41218

ER ST.

CALIFORNIA

1

MOUNT

748 80

The Romulan helmets were cast in rigid rubber, a faster and easier method than the conventional hard plastic and metal. The helmets were also easier to duplicate and more comfortable on the heads of the actors.

NET TOTAL

748 80

Desilu was charged a mere $748.80 for Wah's designing and making the Romulan helmets and ears.

The salt monster, from "The Man Trap,"
is the most memorable of Wah's creatures. Wah's skill infused compassion
and tenderness into the latex mask.

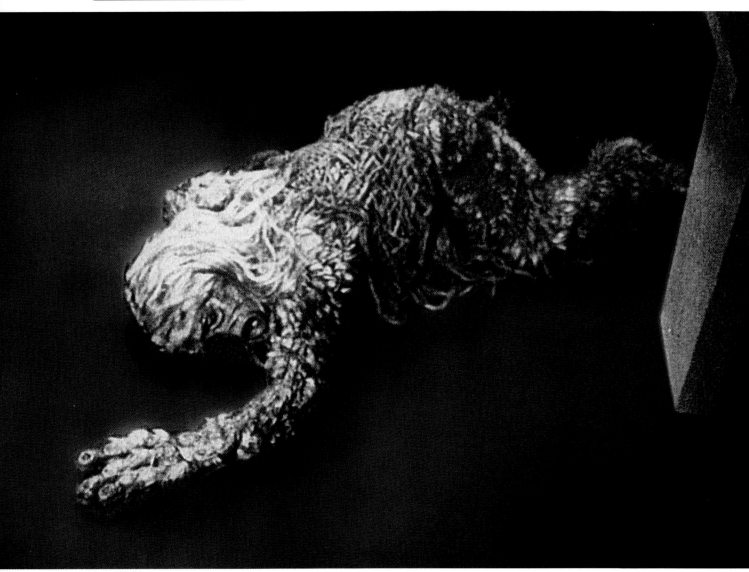

Courtesy Wah Chang

The salt monster, the "co-star," with
William Shatner, of "The Man Trap." This
ad from Wah's own archives was for the
premier episode. However, *Star Trek* was
an NBC show, not ABC, an error that the
newspaper editor obviously missed.

SPACECRAFT STOWAWAY—A crisis erupts aboard the U.S.S. Enterprise when an alien life form, which like a chameleon, is able to change its appearance at will, runs amok threatening ship and crew including its commander Captain James T. Kirk (William Shatner) in "The Man Trap" on Star Trek, Thursday, 8:30 PM, on ABC.

★   ★   ★

243

Courtesy Wah Chang

Paramount Pictures

The final version of Balok. This shot was chosen
as the background for Herbert F. Solow's
"Executive in Charge of Production" credit.

The initial sketch of Balok's
alter ego from "The
Corbomite Maneuver."

The Gorn created for the episode "Arena." Several pieces are used, not only to facilitate costuming the stuntman, but also to shoot the separate pieces as "inserts." An insert could be a close-up of just the head or hands.

The Gorn unfolds. Note that the legs are the Gorn's, but not yet "colored."

The holes were created in the
jacket to allow for ventilation.

The Gorn realized. With
the addition of the cos-
tume pieces, a "seamless"
alien comes to life.

Wah and Glen Taylor were married in 1942. He credits Glen as a tremendous asset to his career. Glen Chang is playing a Vulcan instrument, one of Wah's creations.

The first appearance of the Vulcan harp, from "Charlie X."

Director Joe Pevney saw a "fluffy ball" at the end of a keychain being sold in a drugstore and decided that should be the look of a tribble. Assigned the project of making the cuddly creatures, Wah made hundreds of small artificial fur bags, stuffed them with foam plastic, and hand-sewed each of them.

Another creature from the workshop of Wah Chang, the aggressive inhabitant of Taurus II, in "The Galileo Seven."

The Romulan spaceship
was designed and built
by Wah Chang.

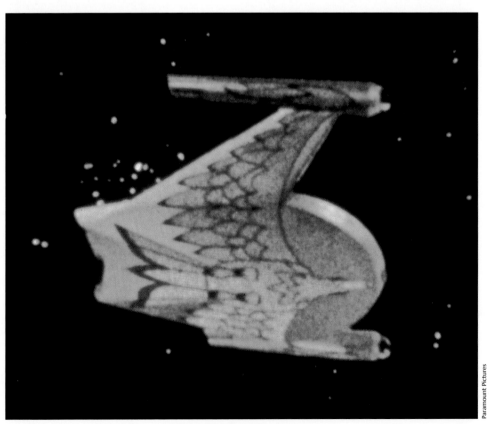

Wah Chang retired from the motion-picture industry in 1970. He built a home in Carmel Valley, California, and concentrated on his first love—sculpting in bronze and marble. An example is seen here: "Polar Bear with Cub II."

WAH MING CHANG RECENTLY CELEBRATED HIS 79TH BIRTHDAY.

253

ACKNOWLEDGMENTS

ARTISTS'

Most creative people readily acknowledge the help of others—both their peers and those in their employ—in accomplishing their work. So it is with Matt, Bill, Freddie, and Wah.

In our research, we have discovered a number of people who deserve to be recognized as significant contributors to our deceased artists' work. If we have omitted anyone, it is not intentional, and we would be happy to be informed for future editions:

BILL THEISS
Geneva Curd, Ken Harvey, Pat Manning, Kirk Templeman, Andrea Weaver.

FRED PHILLIPS
Nina Phillips Coleman, Webster Phillips.

Our living artists have asked us to include with their gratitude the following:

MATT JEFFERIES
Franz Bachelin, Frank Barnett, Rolland "Bud" Brooks, James Clayton, John Dwyer, Pato Guzman, John Jefferies, Joe Jennings, David Marshall, James Rugg, Steve Sardonis, Lew Splittgerber and—Cliffie.

WAH CHANG
John Napolitano.

AUTHORS'

Sincere thanks to these good people who gave us both assistance and advice on the visual world of our original *Star Trek* designers (with particular thanks to the Phillips family for expending tremendous effort in searching the nooks and crannies of their lives and unearthing the past):

Rolland "Bud" Brooks
Glen Chang
Wah Chang
Nina Phillips Coleman
Mary Ann Jefferies
Walter "Matt" Jefferies
Lindsley Parsons, Jr.
Jean Phillips
Kay Brown Phillips
Webster Phillips
Gloria Robertson
Crayton Smith
Dan Striepeke
Kirk Templeman
Shirley Wachter
Andrea Weaver

Thanks to several organizations who saved the past for us to explore:
Costume Design's Guild
   Local 892 IATSE
The Los Angeles Times
The Margaret Herrick Library of the
   Academy of Motion Picture
   Arts and Sciences

And thanks to our editors at Pocket Books, Margaret Clark and Kevin Ryan, who had the idea and asked us to write this book.

254